"To us!"

In loving salute Ross raised his glass to Eileen.

And to love, she added silently. *May it continue forever.*

They each took a sip of champagne, then Ross pulled her into his arms. His lips grazed her bare shoulder, causing a riot of sensation. Eileen shivered. The heady feelings certainly weren't due to the wine....

"I want you," he admitted raggedly. "Oh, Eileen, I want you so very, very much."

"And I want you." Eileen's voice was husky with arousal, and she moved against him seductively. "So let's do something about it...."

THE AUTHOR

Cathy Gillen Thacker began writing novels when her children were toddlers. Now, eight years later, she has had several romances published and thoroughly enjoys her work.

"I believe that love is the one thing people should never have to do without," says Cathy. Happily married with three children, she gets a lot of it herself.

Books by Cathy Gillen Thacker

HARLEQUIN TEMPTATION
47–EMBRACE ME, LOVE

HARLEQUIN AMERICAN ROMANCE
37–TOUCH OF FIRE
75–PROMISE ME TODAY

These books may be available at your local bookseller.

Don't miss any of our special offers. Write to us at the following address for information on our newest releases.

Harlequin Reader Service
P.O. Box 52040, Phoenix, AZ 85072-2040
Canadian address: P.O. Box 2800, Postal Station A,
5170 Yonge St., Willowdale, Ont. M2N 6J3

Embrace Me, Love

CATHY GILLEN THACKER

Harlequin Books

TORONTO • NEW YORK • LONDON
AMSTERDAM • PARIS • SYDNEY • HAMBURG
STOCKHOLM • ATHENS • TOKYO • MILAN

To Jim and Mary Thacker
for their warmth and love over the years.

Published February 1985

ISBN 0-373-25147-5

Printed in Canada

1

"I'M NOT INTERESTED in further excuses. I want re-sults—and I want them today," Eileen Garrett de-manded evenly. "I have customers who have been waiting to close the deal on a house for well over eight weeks, and your department is the only factor holding us up. No, I won't call back on Monday! I need that loan approval now, and I can't possibly get it issued without first having your report."

She sighed, the force of her exasperation clearly carrying over the telephone lines, and still the indo-lent employee's excuses raged on. Eileen's next words were clipped and precise. "Find me your manager, and get him on the line. Now."

One well-manicured hand massaged the tension from her temples, as Eileen leaned back in her conference-room chair, waiting, the telephone re-ceiver cradled next to her ear. Late-morning sun-light spilled in through slatted blinds as the seconds drew out into a full minute. Her feet tapped an im-patient rhythm on the smoothly carpeted floor. In front of her was a list of overdue credit reports as well as assorted papers from the loan-closing she'd just presided over. Frustration pursed her softly glossed lips and lent fire to her hazel eyes, as a sec-ond person came onto the line and repeated an in-different recitation of why the information Eileen had requested was now over two weeks late. Furious with the local credit bureau's habitual incompetence, Eileen ran a hand through her shoulder-length golden-brown hair, restlessly combing the side-swept bangs and the gently curving ends into place. "I don't care what baseball game was on last night or when you held your company picnic or how many employees you have on vacation! I've had it with you people. I'm lodging a formal complaint." A written reproach from her bank, signed and endorsed by upper management would have to be investigated and answered by the credit union's management. Suddenly it seemed miracles could be worked. A sigh parted Eileen's lips, and she leaned forward in her contoured chair, crossing long lissome legs. The action caused her skirt to ride up slightly, and the smooth line of tailored fabric clung snugly to her slender hips and thighs.

"All right, all right, we'll get them to you by the end of the day," the voice on the other end of the line assured finally in a provokingly unhelpful tone.

"Well, see that you do," she stated shortly, losing her temper at last. "Because I can't do my job until you do yours, and I'm warning you now I won't take the blame for someone else's careless attitude and incompetent work." Scowling, Eileen slammed down the phone.

Tension rippled through her coltish five-foot-seven frame as she stood wearily and began stuffing papers back into the appropriate files. At twenty-nine, Eileen carried herself with an elegant assurance earned through years of hard work and self-sacrifice. Tiny diamond studs adorned her pierced ears, and a single strand of gold laced her neck, teasing the upper circumference of her breasts. Glancing down at her watch, she was not surprised to see that her normal lunch hour had long since passed and her stomach growled hungrily as she moved around the room picking up papers and pens, tossing away half-finished soft drinks and cups of coffee. She swore softly as her stomach rumbled protestingly again. She only had another forty-five minutes until her next scheduled appointment, and, darn it all, she was starving!

Unfortunately, no sooner had she opened the conference-room door than she saw the tall man standing in the American City Bank lobby. An expression of supreme displeasure on his face, he was arguing loudly with a nineteen-year-old teller. Eileen could tell from the stunned expression on the young clerk's face that she was ill-equipped to handle the scene. Worse, everyone else of authority seemed to be gone momentarily, too—probably out to lunch.

"No, no one else will do," the man stated with quiet but convincing authority. A tingle of immediate wariness shot down Eileen's spine. The man seemed to be almost daring the clerk to try to defy him. And although his manner was outwardly genial she sensed within him a temper as strong as her own. One hand was placed casually in the pocket of his trousers, the other resting lightly on the counter. His spine was ramrod straight, his shoulders broad and his waist disarmingly slim. The suit was cut exquisitely with the jacket ending halfway down his hips. The masculine curves revealed were taut and well-rounded, the thighs beneath firmly flexed. Dark sable-brown hair contrasted with the starched white collar of his cotton dress shirt.

He listened to the clerk murmur a response, then interrupted impatiently. "No, that will not do. I want to see Ms Eileen Garrett, not Mr. Rutherford or any other senior loan officer. It's a personal matter, and it needs to be taken care of as swiftly as possible.

Believe me—" his voice lowered with what she supposed was distaste "—I wouldn't be here unless it were absolutely necessary."

Quickly Eileen stepped back out of sight being careful to leave the door to the atrium-styled bank lobby slightly ajar. Personal matter! What was he talking about? She'd never seen that man before in her life.

"My name is Ross Mitchell," the man continued to explain, abruptly switching to a more soothing, reasonable tone. "Surely you must know when she'll be in," he coaxed the girl charmingly, "or at the very least where I can reach her."

Suddenly Eileen knew who he was and what he wanted, and she was determined to avoid him. Honestly, why couldn't the tenacious trial lawyer simply accept the "no" she'd left on his answering machine weeks before? Did he think by talking to her in person he'd change her mind about her son?

Unfortunately, his attempt to seduce the teller into helping was working. "If you'd like to leave a message," Lydia offered with a little more composure, her eyes never leaving the man's handsome face.

"I'd rather not, as Ms Garrett is a world class champion when it comes to not returning calls," he stated pleasantly, making no effort to mask a rather odious sigh. "I will, however, wait."

Oh, bother! Eileen thought. *There goes my lunch hour! Damn the man's persistence anyway.* Now what was she going to do? Hide there forever or just wait until Lydia gave her away? Heaven knew she didn't want to discuss her son with the man at all, and even less so in the lobby of the bank where she worked. She edged closer toward the door, curiosity prompting her to survey him in more detail.

Ross Mitchell was elegantly dressed in a lightweight blue summer suit that emphasized his lithe athletic build. His hair was cropped in precise two-inch layers, a preppy sophisticated style that suited him to perfection. His skin was lightly tanned. From what she could see of his expression it contained the same capable, no-nonsense quality of his voice. The stammering teller hadn't a chance under his steady gaze.

"Well, j-just a minute," Lydia finally capitulated. "I'll...see what I can find out for you." With a flurry of movement and the clatter of too-high heels, she threaded her way past other employees and patrons to the conference room beyond.

Eileen moved behind the door, then waited until Lydia was well in the room before making her presence known. Her fingertips pressed against her lips in a direction of silence, Eileen hissed commandingly, "Ask if anyone's seen me, and do it loud enough so Ross Mitchell will hear!"

Lydia glanced at Eileen as if the twenty-nine-year-old loan officer had lost her mind, but she cleared her throat obediently. "Uh...has anyone seen Eileen?"

An Academy Award winner she was not. Eileen rolled her eyes at the unmistakable wariness in the younger employee's voice. Her hands against her mouth, Eileen faked a throaty but audible negative reply, then drew Lydia closer. They stood out of sight of the door, relaxing only slightly. Lydia hissed at once, "Eileen, what's going on?"

Eileen ventured a quick look through the quarter-inch crack around the hinges of the door. Ross Mitchell was still waiting impatiently, glancing at the spacious interior of the Indianapolis bank lobby. "Ross Mitchell's been trying to speak to me for weeks now, but I've been so busy I haven't had time to get back to him." *Or maybe you just didn't want to talk to him,* an inner voice chided. *Maybe you were afraid he would persuade you, or at the very least destroy all your arguments.* She swallowed, continuing, "He wants Teddy to join his Little League team."

Lydia's shoulders sagged in disappointment. "Oh, is that all?" Her glance narrowed appraisingly. "Well, whether Teddy joins the team or not, why won't you at least talk to him? What could it possibly hurt?"

Me, she thought. "Lydia, I don't have the time, energy or inclination to argue with him. It would just be a verbal volleyball match." And she disliked being cross-examined by one of the state's best attorneys. Eileen frowned, defensively crossing her arms across her chest.

"He does look awfully determined," Lydia mused.

"All lawyers are, and sports enthusiasts are the worst. They get bent on winning all the time, no matter what the cost." Anxious to remove herself from the premises, Eileen glanced at her watch, noting she had just thirty minutes until her next appointment. "Look, I've got to have some lunch or I'm going to faint from sheer hunger." She lied, for in her agitation her appetite had all but vanished. "Do me a favor and keep Ross Mitchell in the lobby until I can make a safe getaway."

"What shall I tell him?"

Quickly Eileen gathered up her purse and keys and locked the papers in a nearby file for safekeeping until she could properly file them away. "Just say I've gone out, flip through the calendar on my desk and after a lot of hemming and hawing make an appointment for late next week." She could always cancel it later, on his home phone-answering machine, rather than speak with him directly. "Tell him absolutely nothing else is available—I'm booked solid."

"But if there is anything open earlier—" The conscientious Lydia wavered.

"Tell him, anyway." It wasn't like her to run from confrontations, or force polite business lies on others. Eileen preferred to deal in a straightforward manner. But this was an exception, she told herself firmly. Her son's well-being was at stake.

"Okay, Eileen." Lydia sighed, sensing her friend wasn't going to budge. "But if you ask me, you're making a gargantuan mistake! The man's gorgeous!"

"So I've noticed," Eileen said dryly. *So what?*

Lydia returned to the lobby, and Eileen left the conference room via a side exit and slipped out the back entrance of the bank.

The tree-shaded employees' parking lot was quiet as she strode out the door toward her bright-green Volkswagen Rabbit sedan. On the surface there was no reason she should be going to such lengths to avoid Ross Mitchell, Eileen supposed. It was the subject of baseball she wanted to avoid and the disturbing thought that her son, Teddy, might, under Ross Mitchell's persuasive tutelage, somehow want to follow in the footsteps of his father.

Her hand was on the handle when the sound of rapid, determined footsteps brought her head up. Ross Mitchell was striding resolutely across the pavement. His mouth curled up at both corners when their gazes collided, but the expression of amusement did not reach his eyes. "Going somewhere, Ms Garrett?" he asked in a tight, fierce voice.

Oh, fiddlesticks! With effort, she cleared her throat, stammering, "How did you—"

"Lucky guess," he enunciated through gritted

teeth. Swiftly his eyes made a tour of her voluptuous body before coming back to settle on the newly flushed planes of her oval face. His brilliant gaze seemed to bore into hers, the effect he was having on her weakening her knees. He moved nearer, halting just inches from her face. Leaning forward, he imparted in a proud soft voice, laced with sarcasm, "I asked your 'gofer' what kind of car you might be driving, just in case I saw it in the lot. So it wasn't hard to figure out who was trying to make such a hasty retreat. And then you do have your son's coloring and eyes, or maybe it's the other way around. Not that I wouldn't have recognized your voice from the recording you left on my answering-machine tape."

Embarrassment hued her cheeks. Her instincts had been right. The man really didn't pull any punches! Haughtily she met his gaze. "I have a previous appointment for which I'm already late, as I'm sure you've been told," she informed him icily.

He grinned, suddenly the pleasantly amused male, and somehow seemed twice as unsettling. "Yeah, I know. Lunch." His eyes caressed the mussed ends of her hair before returning thoughtfully to her face. "Why not let me buy it?" he asked kindly. "We can talk while we eat. I'm hungry, too."

The offer seemed sincere. Rankled by the contentiousness of his manner earlier, however, as well as her own uncharacteristically cowardly behavior, she yanked open the car door and tossed her purse inside. "No thanks, Mr. Mitchell. You see, I don't think we have anything to discuss."

Before she could turn and slide in behind the wheel, he was next to her, one palm resting flatly on the roof of her car, blocking her entrance. "Wrong again, Ms Garrett." He quietly emphasized her name, a swift

visual check of her ring finger on her left hand con-
firming her single status. "Because we have plenty to
discuss. Whether we do it now or at some point in the
future, I assure you, our talk will be had."

Like hell it will! she thought angrily. She hated it
when men tried to push her around by virtue of
their strength and sexual difference. Although he
wasn't touching her in any way, she knew it would
be pointless to try to evade him. A physical struggle
in public would only embarrass them both, and undoubtedly he would win. She'd never so much as get
her key in the ignition until he had his say.

Predictably, as soon as he had her attention, Ross
Mitchell wasted no time with amenities. "I want
your son, Teddy, to join my Little League team," he
snapped out.

"So Teddy told me," she replied, deliberately being as haughty as he was abrupt.

"Then you've talked to your son?" Relief mel-
lowed his tone. His posture became less tense.

Eileen gave him a saber-edged glance. "Only after
you'd already given him your one-for-the-Gipper
routine. Honestly, Mr. Mitchell, don't you think you
might have consulted me about whether or not I
wanted him to play Little League baseball before you
approached Teddy about joining the team?"

"There would have been no point if the child
didn't want to himself," Ross pointed out dryly.

Eileen glared up at him. It was impossible not to
be impressed by the strong oval jawline, the clearly
defined cheekbones and straight, well-formed nose.
Up close, his eyes were a breathtaking turquoise
sparked with deeper emerald-green lights, his eyelashes the same luxuriant sable brown as his hair.
All in all, it was a face meant to make a woman's
heart melt, and for that reason especially she re-

sisted the magnetic pull, the faint stirrings of infatuation and feminine interest. She glanced away, the toe of her bone sling-back pump tapping the pavement.

"There's no point in discussing Teddy's joining your team now, either," she said succinctly, "as I'm not interested or amenable to the idea, and we both know if I don't sign a permission slip Teddy can't play or even practice with the league."

Ross caught her arm above the elbow before she could escape into the safety of her car. "I don't know what you've got against men, whether it's a personal vendetta or some misguided new form of women's lib," he began, insolently perusing her slender body. Despite his infuriatingly chauvinistic words, heat flamed within her, making every cell and nerve ending rebelliously aware of his commanding touch. Her toes curled in her shoes, the muscles of her calves strained against the silken texture of her sheer summer stockings. She hated her reaction, the unnamed awareness he sparked within her, but was powerless to prevent it.

But Ross Mitchell was still muttering accusations as hot-temperedly as ever. "Or what rankles you about softball or your son's predilection for organized sports," he continued scathingly, ignoring the hot flush of color that flooded her cheeks. "But I'm telling you now that your son has a natural talent—"

Shock cut through her fury, whitening her face, making her heart skip several beats. "How do you know that?" Eileen's voice cut sharply across his. Without warning he, too, seemed taken aback. His gaze dropped to the short tailored jacket and softly gathered skirt of her yellow suit, the lacy white boat-necked sweater, and the single strand of gold teasing her breasts before returning to her face. Despite her fury, she'd never been more aware of the fullness of her breasts—grown even more pronounced since Teddy's birth—the nip of her waist, the lush firm plane of her hips.

"I've seen Teddy play baseball," Ross admitted simply, both hands dropping to his sides. *Oh damn, damn, and double damn!* she thought, suddenly defeated. *The man knows how much talent Teddy has, he really knows!* Nervously, she wet her lips. He followed the movement with his interested gaze, then explained matter-of-factly, voice gentler, "I dropped by your sister Janey's to pick up Brian. As you probably know, her son already plays on my team." Knowing he'd finally forced her to listen to what he had to say, Ross straightened. "Teddy was there, and the three of us threw a few softballs. Don't get your dander up," he cut in before she could protest, wagging a long tanned index finger in her face. "It was no big deal, but I meant what I said, Ms Garrett. Your son shows a lot of promise."

So had his father. Recalling what had happened to Ted, Sr., when he'd encountered the unrelenting pressure of the pros, she responded tersely, "Exactly the point, Mr. Mitchell. Teddy does have a very bright future ahead of him." If she could only keep him safe from harassment or undue scrutiny while he was growing up—at least until he was mature enough to have a fighting chance against the legacy of failure his father had left. "But it won't include Little League." Before Ross could open his mouth, she finished icily, "Furthermore, I'd appreciate it if you wouldn't bother either me or my son again." Gathering as much dignity as she could muster, she slid into her car.

Ross stared at her as if she were even more heartless than he'd originally thought. Shaking his head in disapproval, he stepped back as the engine of her Volkswagen roared to life.

Her hands were trembling as she drove away. Eileen told herself firmly it was anger unnerving her so. Her trembling had nothing to do with Ross Mitchell's magnetic presence, the sensual curve of his mouth, the expressive arch of his brows as they mirrored his mood, or the gentle way he had held her arm, even in anger. True, he was a compelling man, successful, undoubtedly extremely virile, well-known for his community activism. But he was also a meddler, she thought, her fist pounding the steering wheel, breasts heaving in agitation. She wouldn't let him interfere further in her life. She wouldn't let him interfere in Teddy's. She could only hope he had at last seen how fruitless his quest was and had given up.

THE REST OF THE AFTERNOON PASSED without incident. Eileen processed several loan applications, opened an IRA account for a self-employed writer and had the unpleasant job of telling a very nice young couple their request for mortgage money had not been approved. She then discussed several viable alternatives for the disappointed newlyweds, such as looking for a house in a less expensive neighborhood, selling one of their two cars to pay off existing credit-card charges or simply waiting another year or two until their salaries were up and interest rates went down. Still, the couple left in a very dejected frame of mind, the young bride on the verge of tears. Their unhappiness stayed with Eileen as she helped close up the branch for the day. Adding to that irritation was the fact that the credit bureau had not come through with the promised report, forcing her to go ahead with the complaint, which might very well end with someone getting fired. Exhausted, she drove to her sister's home to pick up her nine-year-old son.

"So letting Teddy play ball with Ross Mitchell was a mistake," Janey Deveraux concluded minutes later over a glass of iced tea. A mother of four children herself, Janey sometimes had trouble understanding Eileen's overwhelming need to protect her son. "How was I to know he'd want to draft Teddy for his team?"

Eileen looked at Janey's halo of auburn curls, the composed expression on her lovely face, and wished she had some of her older sister's serenity. "You know how I feel about Teddy finding out about his father." Especially that Ted, Sr., had been anything less than perfect.

"Ross is a responsible man," Janey reminded her sternly. Casually, she checked and stirred the pan of aromatic strawberry preserves simmering on the stove. Although eight years apart in age, the two sisters had always been close. And there had been times, Eileen had to admit, that she had needed Janey desperately. When Ted had died, Eileen had been three months pregnant. Janey had coached her through the Lamaze classes and the birth of her son, then cared for Teddy all day so Eileen could go back to work. Janey was her best friend and confidante, but she was also her severest critic, and right now Eileen could see the gentle censure in Janey's eyes. But Janey's vast experience in homemaking and motherhood didn't allay Eileen's fears in this instance. She'd never had to go through a personal experience as tragic as Ted's death had been; she didn't have to deal with the fact the fatal car accident should never have taken place—wouldn't have, if

Eileen had just been a more understanding and intuitively aware wife.

Eileen pushed back her chair and glanced out the window to where the other children were playing touch football on the lawn. "Ross might be responsible—but other coaches might not. And if they let it be known to the press that Ted's son has joined the local Little League, there's no telling what will happen." Certainly it would dredge up the scandal surrounding Ted's death and the unhappy times preceding it. Eileen didn't think she could bear to suffer through any more guilt. She didn't want to chance losing her son's love because of a situation she'd been too young and inexperienced to handle.

Silence fell between the women. "All right." Janey sighed, moving restlessly to the window crammed with geraniums. "I won't press you on the issue. I know what a tough time you had with reporters when Ted died." Nearly a year had passed before the pressure let up and Eileen had been allowed to fade quietly into obscurity to lead a normal life.

Janey surveyed Eileen fondly. Gently, she changed the subject. "You look exhausted. Why don't you and Teddy stay for dinner?"

Eileen wanted to, but she said, "Janey, we've imposed so many times...and had you over in return so few."

"Oh, are you going to start that again? You know I don't mind. Dinner's already prepared. You know we always have plenty. I routinely cook enough to feed an army. So what do you say? It's just an informal barbecue in the backyard. We don't plan to eat for a couple of hours, so you'll even have time to run home and change."

It was a persuasive argument. Eileen relented, remembering the lunch she'd been too keyed up to eat.

"I never could resist your cooking." Janey made every meal a culinary feast. "What would you like me to bring?"

"How about dessert?"

"I'll stop by the bakery on the way back," Eileen promised, reaching for her car keys. "Anything in particular you'd like me to get?"

Janey shook her head. "Just something for the children. You know how deprived they feel if they don't end every backyard picnic in the grandest of style."

Eileen laughed. A barbecue without a brownie was no picnic at all.

"Leave Teddy here," Janey suggested as her sister headed for the door. "It will be faster."

"You're sure?" Eileen asked.

Janey stared down into the playpen where her youngest, an auburn-haired toddler, slept. She reached down to tenderly smooth a wisp of sleep-damp hair from the little girl's cheek. "When you have four children, and the oldest are teenage twins, one more child is no big deal. Besides, Teddy will keep Brian out of trouble, or vice versa."

Or get each other into dutch, Eileen thought, recalling some of their more elaborate and mischievous schemes. "Thanks."

The two sisters exchanged a heartfelt grin and hug. "Anytime," Janey bantered. "Now, scoot!"

As ALWAYS, a talk with her sister had calmed Eileen down. She was in much better spirits as she drove the short distance home. For the past three years, she and Teddy had lived in a small two-bedroom condominium in the heart of suburban Indianapolis. Only three blocks from Janey's, Eileen's home was her largest investment and the one she was most proud of. While having all the tax advantages of home ownership, she didn't have the chore of cutting the grass and maintaining the outside of the building. Rather, she paid a monthly association fee for those chores. Unfortunately the yards weren't as spacious as those in Janey's neighborhood, and there weren't many other children for Teddy to play with. But it was the best she could do, and she strove to make it as much a real, permanent home for them as possible.

Blue-gray wallpaper decorated the living room and entryway, plush burgundy pile carpeted the floor. Her furniture was of the finish-it-yourself variety, all antiqued in a polished mahogany hue and coated with a protective substance for longer wear. Her sofa and armchairs had been picked up at a local auction. Eileen had spent a full-week's salary having them re-covered in a stain-repellent oatmeal white. A small color television sat against the wall. Bookshelves were built in on both sides of the muted-rose brick fireplace. Eileen had filled the dark wood shelves with a few cherished mementos as well as volumes of books she and Teddy could both enjoy.

Her mind on the evening ahead, Eileen swept through the darkened hall, through the living room, to the master bedroom upstairs. Tossing off her business attire, she went to the closet and pulled on a pair of freshly laundered designer jeans, white cotton athletic socks and sneakers and a vibrant red cotton shirt with mandarin collar and button front, worn open at the throat. She paused before the mirror only long enough to run a brush through her hair, pinning one side of the gently curling length behind her ear. Humming softly to herself, she sprayed on cologne, brushed her teeth, washed her face, applied lip gloss and blush. Satisfied with her appearance and feeling much fresher, she started back down the steps. The doorbell rang as she hit the bottom step. Sighing her exasperation at the delay, Eileen moved to get it.

She opened the door to the devastatingly attractive face of Ross Mitchell. He'd been leaning on the door, one bent elbow resting on the frame, but his arm dropped and he straightened languidly when he saw her. His smile widened appreciatively as their eyes met. She noted he'd removed his tie and undone the first few buttons on his crisp white shirt. The overall effect was casually urbane and relaxed. More infuriating than his arrogant ease was the fact he seemed to be waiting—no, to expect—to be invited in! And after the way they had parted, too!

"What are you doing here?" Eileen's frosty voice erased his pleased expression.

He shrugged and stepped past her, ignoring her halfhearted attempt to block his way in. "I was going to say 'apologize' but now that I'm here, I don't think that's what I want at all." He glanced back toward the street. She saw a shining black Mercedes at the curb. "Is it all right to park there, I wonder?" he asked, brow furrowing.

"I don't see why not," she retorted crisply, "as you won't be staying long." He laughed, and the sound reverberated deep in his throat. Her gaze was drawn back to his shirt. She saw the curling dark brown hairs escaping the parted cloth, the tanned hue of his skin. A thrill went through her, escalating her rage—this time as much at herself as at him. "What do you want?" Fire thrummed in her temples, warring with the icy reserve in her veins. Why wouldn't he leave her alone?

Ross glanced up at the cooling jet of air coming from the air-conditioning duct overhead, then reached around behind him and shut the door. They faced each other across the red-tiled entryway, but she deliberately made no move to invite him in farther.

"We didn't finish our conversation this afternoon," he continued smoothly.

Eileen followed his glance to her chest, very aware that the thin red cotton outlined her breasts to their best advantage and that her jeans, though comfortable and worn, were similarly adhering to her thighs, flat stomach and the taut curve of her buttocks. She wished she still had on heels. Her flat-soled running shoes made her feel shorter, younger and hence more vulnerable. For just a moment, Ross's gaze rested on her, noting the color in her cheeks and the newly brushed shimmer of her hair.

"I said everything I had to say." Her tone was as flat and as uninviting as she could make it.

Ross's smile became less patient. Hands on his hips, he stalked closer, his still-reasonable tone in direct contrast to his predatory air. "Look, my team needs a first-rate hitter badly. If what I saw at Janey's the other day is any indication, Teddy's skills alone could put my boys in the running for the league's division championship, maybe even send them on to state. Won't you at least consider it?" He paused, finally adding, after swallowing with difficulty, "Please?"

From the way he was acting he might as well have been down on his hands and knees. But his beseeching attitude did nothing to cover the fact that the man was an opportunist. As casually as she could, she introduced the subject of her late husband. "I assume this means you're aware Teddy's father played professional baseball." She watched Ross carefully, alert for any sign of guilty reaction on his part.

He hesitated, stepping back slightly in his shock. "No, as a matter of fact, I wasn't aware of that." Ross shrugged his shoulders uncaringly. His gaze impaled her thoughtfully. "Now that you mention it, though, the name Garrett does seem familiar." He ran the edge of his index finger thoughtfully across his lower lip, drawing her unwilling attention to how soft it looked in contrast to the rugged rest of him. She wondered whimsically how he would kiss, then with a start banished the thought from her mind.

The last thing Eileen wanted was for him to jog any recollection of Ted, Sr., or—heaven forbid—dig through any old newspaper files. Reluctantly she enlightened him, whirling around to face the hall mirror. "Ted was named All-American his junior year at Purdue." She touched her hair lightly in an attempt to cover her nervousness and avoid his scrutiny. "He played for the Cincinnati Reds briefly before he died."

Ross stepped behind her. The warmth of his breath caressed her shoulders. His eyes met hers in the mirror. "What position?" There was only deadly seriousness on his face now, that and the quest to find out more about her, why she was acting this way.

Eileen swallowed, dropping her eyes and turning away. She pivoted, moving restlessly across the hall, only her footsteps breaking the silence that fell. She could hear his breathing and hers, knowing that they were very much alone. Perspiration dampened her palms. "Shortstop."

"I see." Straightening, he sighed, his manner becoming more formal. "I'm sorry if I appeared insensitive. I did know you were a widow. Beyond that, nothing." He paused, as if trying to decipher if she was still carrying a torch for Ted. Eileen stared at him blankly, refusing to clue him in. *Maybe it would be better this way,* she thought silently, *if he thought that, let that keep him away.* Heaven knew, despite her anger, how susceptible she seemed to his presence.

"But don't you see? That's all the more reason for Teddy to play," Ross finished, his voice like a whisper of black velvet floating over her bare skin.

Only memories, haunting and hurtful, kept her decision firm. She whirled away, tears blurring her eyes. "I don't want my son pressured unduly." She composed herself, whirled and gave Ross a warning glare, feeling suddenly about as hospitable as a mother bear whose cub had been threatened by a stalking hunter. *Please,* she thought. *Give up. Go away. Leave me alone.*

"He won't be pressured. Not if he's on my team." Pointedly, he ignored her wordless attempt to dismiss him.

Her brows rose in cool, angry disbelief. "And yet if I'm to go by what you said earlier, Mr. Mitchell—" she laced her voice with all the soft sarcasm she could muster "—you're already relying on Teddy's batting skills to put your team in the running for division championship."

Ross frowned, a flush staining his neck as he recalled his words. "Ms Garrett, I didn't mean that literally. I have plenty of other talented boys on the team, too, including your sister's son. I just wanted to get across the amount of potential I think your son has. I certainly haven't said anything of the kind to Teddy."

She grinned ruefully, unconvinced. "Expectations have a way of transmitting themselves, nonetheless." No one knew better than Teddy's father had, and Eileen now lived constantly with the results. "I'm sorry." She brushed past Ross toward the door. "But having Teddy play Little League is out of the question."

"Even if it's what his father would have wanted?" His silken taunt caught her as no physical motion ever could have.

"That's hitting below the belt, wouldn't you say?" she accused harshly. Eileen turned toward him, the color draining from her face.

"No less so than your low opinion of me," he reiterated smoothly, taking a definitive step nearer. "And just as unjust."

Her back grazed the door. "You don't know what Ted would've wanted," she began emotionally. "And for you to even presume to suggest—" Her voice broke off. She knew that Ross was right, it was what Teddy's father would have wanted for him. But it still would have been a mistake. She was silent, staring at the floor.

"Then explain it to me so I do understand," he implored gently, his eyes never leaving her face.

But she couldn't, not without making herself even more vulnerable to him. In response he moved closer, until they were standing only inches apart, her head tilted up toward him, her eyes averted. They were near enough to gauge the meter of each other's breath. She could see the slight shadow of a day's growth of beard lining his jaw and knew he could inhale freely the jasmine of her perfume. Suddenly she felt trapped, threatened and more in danger, both sensually and emotionally, than she had ever been in her life. Her fear was that Ross, by studying her long enough, would somehow read her thoughts, be privy to the dark secrets she alone knew. Instinctively, she put a hand up, as if to halt his scrutiny. Shaking his head in silent refusal, he moved closer still. Her fingertips grazed his lapel— her forearm wedging distance between them—then stilled, resting lightly on the linen fabric of his coat. Her eyes narrowed to the loosened button of his collar, the crisp dark hair fluffing out from the edges of his shirt, the tantalizing surface of the tanned skin beneath it. She swayed slightly as a secret and unwanted thrill shot through her. "I promise you the experience will be a positive one for Teddy," he said, his voice low. It was as if he were promising to help her, as well.

Their gazes collided again, held. Suddenly, her son was no longer her primary concern. She was afraid for herself, afraid Ross would move closer still, that his mouth would lower and his lips would graze hers. More devastating than the action was the knowledge she would very probably respond, not mildly or acquiescently, but wantonly and with all her heart and soul. It wasn't like her to give in to infatuation, to fantasize, no matter how devastating a man's physical presence. And yet, even now, she could ....

Flexing her hand slightly, Eileen shoved against the muscled surface of his chest and slipped past. "Next you'll be trying to tell me organized sports build character," she joked weakly, strolling toward the leafy green plant on the parson's table decorating the hall. The philodendron was badly in need of both water and pruning.

He followed, frowning as he, too, took in the disgraceful condition of the plant. "Sports do build character." He moved to lounge genially against the wall. His gaze trailed lazily over her, noting the snug fit of her jeans at the vee of her thighs, the neckline of her blouse, the way the shirt softly molded her breasts. She flushed. He went on, appearing not to notice the high color in her cheeks. "Sports also teach a boy the value of team effort, how to win, lose and never give up, to expect and get the very best of himself. Teddy needs that, Eileen, and it's something that you alone can't give him, not now, not ever."

Ross Mitchell believed every word he said. His sincerity made her ashamed for ever doubting his motives. "Maybe in a few years then," Eileen relented softly. When Teddy was old enough to deal with the truth about his father and the reasons for his short-lived career and untimely death.

Ross straightened. "Look, I can understand why you'd want to protect your son. He's all you have left of your husband. But in a few years, athletically, he'll be that much further behind his peers." Her head shot up at the criticism, and he finished with blunt honesty. "I said Teddy's got talent. I didn't say he knew how to pitch, field, slide into a base or even hit so much as a ground ball." Ross paused. "The fact of the matter is, Teddy asked me to talk to you, to try and convince you to let him play. That's why I'm here. Because I promised him I would."

Not because, as she'd initially presumed, Ross's team couldn't survive without Teddy. Or even because he was somehow inexplicably drawn to her, as she was to him.

Blind astonishment robbed her temporarily of speech. She'd always tried to be supportive, to somehow make up for the fact Teddy had no father. Never, to her knowledge, had her son felt the need to go to anyone else. The realization that he had gone to Ross, a stranger, hurt. Even worse was her own attraction to the maddeningly attractive lawyer.

"For the record, I understand your son's dilemma," Ross went on compassionately, as if sensing the depth of her distress. "He obviously loves and respects you. But he also has an intense desire to play softball. If he were my son, I'd let him. Hell," he said gruffly, exasperatedly, lifting both arms in heated emphasis, "I'd go to every game."

She knew he would. Numbly, Eileen walked toward the living room, no longer caring if he stayed. She sank down in a chair, hoping to steady her shaking legs. Ross followed, taking a seat on the sofa. "Why is this so important to you?" she asked quietly. The city held dozens of other eligible boys. Boys whose mothers would welcome Ross's concern.

Ross leaned forward, his hands clasped loosely between his knees. "Perhaps because Teddy and I share similar experiences. My father died when I was barely learning to walk. More than anything, my mother wanted to protect me. Suffice it to say—" Ross's lip curled ironically "—Little League and all such 'dangerous' activities were out for me, too. The most I could do was play kickball or soccer in the back lot, and that was only when she wasn't around." He grinned, shrugging off his deviltry. "Don't get me wrong, my mother was a wonderful woman, just slightly overprotective. But as inconsequential as that sounds, that can be very rough on a boy. I know! Anyway, when I reached high school I finally convinced her to let me compete with the rest and did my damnedest to catch up. Football, basketball, softball—you name it, I tried out for the team. Unfortunately, I was already years behind the other guys in training and practice, and consequently I spent the bulk of my time on the bench. I also missed out on all the athletic scholarships. I'd hate to see that happen to Teddy."

Eileen was silent, absorbing Ross's words. Had he

known that was another of her worries, being able
to pay for Teddy's education? Or had her son confided that about her, too. "Thank you for telling me
this, Mr. Mitchell." She rose and graciously ushered
him to the door. But once she was there, the emotional impact of all he'd said combined with the
misery of her past marriage to hit her like a sledge-
hammer. Tears shimmered treacherously in her eyes.
Where had she gone wrong, that Teddy couldn't even
come to her with his problems? Was this the type of
masculine dilemma for which only another man
would do? And if so, why hadn't her son gone to his
uncle, whom he saw nearly every day? It hurt her
deeply that Teddy had no father to confide in, but she
wouldn't let Ross Mitchell see how miserably she had
failed her son.

"Even if I were amenable to Teddy's joining the
team, it would be impossible, at least as far as this
season goes. I've arranged for him to spend several
weeks in July with his grandparents on their farm,"
Eileen explained.

Ross waved his hand dismissingly before she
could finish. "Everyone has vacations."

She smiled. "In August he'll be spending two
weeks with Ted's family in Florida." Equal time for
everyone, and a summer of sunshine and fun for
Teddy, unhampered by the fact that she worked.

"I see." Ross paused, studying her intently. "It
sounds like Teddy does have a busy summer. Still,
there's no reason he can't practice with the rest of the
boys and at least begin to enjoy and learn about the
sport."

"But the season's already started," she protested,
wishing there were some way she could back away,
put more of a physical distance between herself and
the attractive attorney.

Ross dug through his pants pocket and pulled out his car keys. "I'll coach him privately, spend as much time as necessary to see he's at least caught up with the other new players. At least promise me you'll think about it," he urged.

Her pulse throbbed in reaction to his nearness. Reluctantly she nodded her head. Pleasure softened the etched planes of his face, spinning a new web of danger around them. A speculative light shimmered in his eyes. "So," he asked teasingly, "what will you be doing while Teddy's gone? Got anything special planned to while away those lonely days and nights?" It was an innocent question, meant to put her at ease. It worked like concentrated aphrodisiac pouring into her veins.

She flushed. To speak around the huskiness in her throat was an effort. "I don't have anything special planned." Watch it. Next he'll be volunteering to fill up the nocturnal hours.

The corners of his mouth tilted up slightly. "Seeing anyone in particular?" He moved closer, stopping just short of her.

"Ah—no." She was aware of the dimness of the room. The heavy blue-velvet draperies and fashionable miniblinds had all been drawn against the sun. The soft whir of the air conditioner obliterated all outside sounds. Her breathing seemed as erratic and undependable as her thoughts, her awareness of him unnervingly acute. "Most of the time I'll be working," she finished more composedly, wishing he would go or at least move back slightly. As it was she was trapped against the door, her hand on the knob, without even enough room to pull it open. She could see the laugh lines around his eyes, the wry amusement on his face and realized that despite his incredible poise he was only a few years older than she, maybe thirty-four or thirty-five, and at the moment all waiting rapacious male. Suddenly, he was no longer behaving like a coach interested in recruiting her son. Rather, he was a virile man on the lookout for a woman to take home to his bed. Why had she let him in the house?

"Besides working, what do you have planned?" His free hand rested loosely on his waist.

"I have a lot of reading to get caught up on." She gestured toward her sagging houseplant. "As you can no doubt see, a lot of gardening, too."

He laughed. The humorous exchange broke the sensual tension between them. "Need any help?" he offered, his mouth curving into a generous smile. "I'm no expert, but I do have a rather nice garden and greenhouse of my own."

"Thanks, but I take all my plants to Janey," Eileen stated, relieved to have an easy truthful out, on that score.

But Ross only grinned as he corrected implacably, "And she's been known to get advice from me—at least since Brian joined the team."

"Oh." She felt herself flush, but had no comeback for his suggestion. Ross reached into his pocket, withdrew a printed business card and pressed it warmly into her palm.

"Let me know if you decide to let Teddy play ball and are willing to sign the forms. I'd very much like to have him on my team. As for the plants—"

"I'll call if my efforts to revive them fail." *Maybe. If I'm either terribly desperate or terribly brave.*

He glanced back at the philodendron. His mouth quirked wryly. "Better not wait too long," he teased. "That philly looks terminal."

Unfortunately, it was true. Eileen opened the front door and ushered him out. She accidentally touched the hard swell of muscle above his elbow in the process. Disturbed, she dropped her hand as rapidly as if she'd been burned. His eyes moved over her, his hand took hers in a lazy goodbye clasp. "Good day, Mr. Mitchell," she said firmly, disengaging her palm with difficulty when it appeared he still wanted to linger and chat.

He paused, then shrugged. "Good day, Ms Garrett." Placing both hands in his pockets, he pivoted and strolled jauntily toward his car. She wondered a moment, shivering despite the heat, at his light-hearted mood. He was as victorious as if she'd agreed to let Teddy play on his team. And she hadn't decided anything of the kind. Rather, to the contrary.

With effort Eileen willed away her unease. In all likelihood she'd never see the man again, at least not on a one-to-one basis, even if she did eventually relent and let Teddy play on his team. There was no reason to think about him further. But of course she did. As the minutes passed and he drove away, she found herself able to think about absolutely nothing and no one else.

2

"TEDDY, WHY DIDN'T YOU just tell me how much you wanted to play softball," Eileen began gently, drawing her son down beside her on the cushioned glider. He was getting so tall, she mused. Bright spots of color flushed his cheeks. "I would have understood. We could have at least talked about it."

Dusk descended slowly over the Deveraux's flagstone patio. The redwood picnic table was covered with a red-and-white-checked tablecloth. Packages of rolls, paper plates, silverware, napkins, salt and pepper and condiments were all neatly arranged on the aluminum folding table that served as a portable buffet. A cooler of icy beverages, both beer and soft drinks, sat in the corner. The coals glowed nearly white in the bottom of the black barbecue grill. Soon Janey's husband, Hugh, would be out to start charbroiling the hamburgers and steaks, but for the moment Eileen and her young son were alone. She desperately needed to talk to him, to understand where their communication had failed.

Teddy brushed a shock of sunbleached white-blond hair from his brilliant blue eyes. "Oh, mom, get serious," he said between thirsty gulps of chilled grape juice. He wiped his mouth with the back of his small dusty hand. "I know how much you hate baseball. You won't even watch it on television. Besides, I heard what you said to Aunt Janey when she tried to talk you into signing me up for the league last spring.''

Vaguely, Eileen recalled muttering a facetious but heartfelt ''When Teddy's one hundred and fifty-two and able to take care of himself, maybe!'' She hadn't been aware Teddy was in earshot and would have given anything if he hadn't been. ''You still want to play softball, don't you?''

''Yes.'' He glanced at her steadily. Evidently he read her dismay at his answer, for the corners of his mouth turned down in a sullen pout. His frown deepening, he glowered over at the game of freeze tag still going on out on the lawn.

Eileen sighed. ''Well, maybe next year when we're not so busy you can join Little League,'' she promised finally. ''You can start with the rest of the boys at the beginning of the season. Or maybe play soccer in the fall.''

Her son's jaw clenched. ''I don't want to play soccer. I want to play softball,'' Teddy insisted determinedly. He swiveled toward her, looking so much like his father her heart ached. The seconds strung out between them. Eileen was helpless to explain her feelings as she confronted his scornful gaze. ''I want to be like dad. Why don't you want that, too?''

She swallowed, fighting the tight knot of emotion in her throat, unable to answer. After a moment, she gently shook her head. *No, I can't talk about this, not without crying,* her look said.

Her son sighed, digging the toe of his sneaker into the ground. ''Can I go now?'' Teddy asked impatiently, obviously believing his dream of playing softball would never come true.

After a moment, she relented. ''Sure.'' Eileen watched him race off. Guilt plagued her, but stronger than her son's unhappiness was her fear. What if she did let Teddy play and what if the old scandals were dredged up, her son's view of his father tarnished irrevocably? Would that be worth it? Or was Eileen just delaying the inevitable by not telling Teddy the truth about his father?

Janey walked out the back door, carrying a huge bowl of potato salad in her hands. Hugh followed with a platter of meat and a spatula. He was wearing an apron emblazoned with the words "Kiss the Chef!"

"My, don't you look glum," Janey observed.

Eileen noticed her sister had changed into a hostess skirt and frilly white voile blouse instead of her usual T-shirt and slacks. "I was thinking about Ross Mitchell," she admitted with a resentful scowl. Her discord with Teddy was all his fault. "Damn that man, interfering in my life and dealings with my son!"

Janey and Hugh exchanged a telepathic glance. Janey sighed. "Now, Eileen, Ross is a very nice man."

She snorted inelegantly. "Obviously he has no children of his own to take care of or be responsible for."

Janey tightened the foil over the salad. She and Hugh exchanged another glance. Janey, who was never one to gossip, admitted reluctantly, "Ross was divorced some time ago. He has a son from that marriage. From what I understand they're very close, although his wife has custody."

When Eileen remained wary, Hugh chimed in convincingly, "I've known Ross for several years. We belong to the same civic service club. Ross is tremendously involved with the community, Eileen."

The metal gate clanged shut abruptly. Everyone turned toward the sound. "There's no need for a character reference, Hugh," a gravelly baritone interjected. The voice was accompanied by a pair of intense green eyes and a controlled, polite look on his handsome face.

Ross Mitchell, she thought, as her heart turned over in her chest. His familiar voice sent prickles of sensation rippling across the back of her neck, his presence made her knees rubbery, her palms damp, every sense unerringly acute. Ross Mitchell greeted the Deverauxes with a casual lift of his palm, then favored Eileen with a deliberately relaxed smile as he sauntered into the yard. He stopped to look Eileen up and down, acknowledging her presence with a wordless nod. She felt caged, wary, as if he could see through her every defense far more intimately than could Janey and Hugh. Ross exchanged amenities with the Deverauxes before turning his faintly provoking gaze back toward Eileen. "Ms Garrett."

Judging by Janey's guilty expression, the tenacious trial lawyer had been expected. And Eileen had deliberately not been forewarned! "Mr. Mitchell." Eileen nodded coolly, trying without success to tame the embarrassed color in her cheeks. She could feel her pulse racing and chided herself for having let him affect her this way. He'd changed into a thinly striped blue-green-and-white golf shirt, casual navy slacks and sport shoes. He looked more intent than he had earlier, more muscular, more fit. She forced her eyes away from the sinewy forearms, the dark curling hair that sprang from the open vee of his shirt. Why did he have to be so attractive, his gaze so intense?

In an effort to still her nerves, Eileen sipped at the glass of soda in her hand. The carbonated bubbles fizzed in her throat, nearly refusing to go down.

"Oh now, what's this formality?" Hugh boomed

in the silence that fell. "We're all friends here. Surely we can move things along to a first-name basis."

Ross took a seat opposite hers. "I'm willing if you are." His eyes held hers, and his voice reached out to her, bridging the gardenia-scented space between them.

Eileen shifted uncomfortably. She didn't seem to have much choice if she wasn't going to spoil the party. "All right...Ross," she offered reluctantly. But her display of forced cordiality only seemed to intrigue him more. He leaned forward fractionally in his chair, one palm pressed flat against his thigh. Without warning, Brian and Teddy came charging up to greet their guest. "Hi, Mr. Mitchell!" Teddy shouted exuberantly. "Want to play some softball?"

Ross shot Eileen a quick look and after gauging her reaction begged off politely. "It's a little too close to dinner, don't you think?"

Hugh added firmly, "I agree. Boys, better go wash up. Brian, Teddy, round up the girls." After complaining boisterously, the boys obediently raced off.

"Nice boys," Ross commented. "Rowdy, but nice." He looked at Janey and nodded toward the kitchen. "Can I help you with anything?"

She shook her head. "Eileen, would you see Ross gets a drink? I'm going to go in and get the high chair."

"I'll give her a hand with the baby," Hugh commented, following his wife into the house. Eileen and Ross were left alone. The silence was so intense she could hear the whisper of the summer breeze above the occasional chirping of a cricket or rumbling car engine far away, out on the suburban street. Her throat was so dry it ached. She glanced toward the cooler. "Can I get you a beer?"

But whatever he wanted from her, it was definitely

not to be waited on. "I'll get it," he told her curtly. Rising unceremoniously, Ross removed a beer from the cooler and popped off the tab. "I apologize if my presence here caught you off guard." He gave her a long evaluating look then took a lengthy sip of his beer.

Eileen moved restlessly in her chair, feeling like a total ingrate. The only crime Ross could be accused of was trying to help her son. And how could she hold that against him, knowing as she did that he did not have access to the whole story. Nor was he likely to get it from anyone but her. That, however, did not excuse his duplicity in the set-up dinner. "You knew I was going to be here, though," she guessed.

He nodded. "I called Janey after I got home. I wanted to talk to her about next week's practice schedule. They've changed the times and locations of a couple of games, and she usually alerts the other parents. She mentioned you'd be here only after I already had accepted her dinner invitation."

"I see. I'm sorry." She really hated being fixed up with anyone and imagined he would feel the same.

His teeth flashed white against the tan of his face, and the knowing look he gave her was one of sheer delight. "I'm not."

Fresh color highlighted her cheeks. But try as she might, she could formulate no reply. The clatter of the boys barreling out of the screen door interrupted their staring match. The teenage twins followed, one girl carrying the high chair, the other, baby Amy. Eileen jumped up to help Janey serve the rest of the meal. Both Brian's and Teddy's excitement continued undampened. "Mr. Mitchell's the best baseball coach in the whole world!" Brian exclaimed between bites of buttered corn on the cob.

Eileen spread mustard onto Teddy's second hamburger and added more milk to the baby's plastic drinking cup. Her own meal had barely been touched. "Why is that, Brian?" she asked pleasantly, curious to know what it was about Ross that generated such unchecked adoration of the boys. He did seem to have a good rapport with the children. In truth, she'd never seen Teddy more enamored by an adult male. He hadn't taken his eyes off his "coach" all during dinner.

Brian wiped catsup from the corner of his mouth with the back of his hand then, at his mother's reproachful glare, dabbed at the place where the spot had been with the corner of his napkin. "First of all, he never yells at anyone. Second, he always lets everybody field and bat every single game. On his team, we always take turns so nobody has to sit on the bench."

Ross Mitchell looked decidedly warmer. Enjoying the fact it was his turn to be embarrassed, Eileen prodded her nephew. "Go on."

"Well, he always buys us snowcones after each game, whether we win or lose!" Brian confessed.

"Impressive!" Eileen murmured.

Even in the dusky light, it appeared coach Mitchell's cheeks were growing brighter, as were the very tips of his ears. He studied the redwood fence. "And he never misses a practice or makes us work out with an assistant coach," Brian continued enthusiastically. "He goes to every single game."

Hugh interrupted, "Brian, how about more potato salad?"

"Nah...uh, no thank you, I'm full," Brian amended, remembering his manners.

"Better," Hugh said, casting his son a more approving glance.

Eventually, the children asked to be excused.

Janey went in to give Amy a bath. Hugh mumbled something about hunting up spare containers for the fireflies the boys planned to catch. The teenage twins were off to a dance at the YWCA. Feeling somewhat more relaxed, Eileen and Ross companionably scraped the plates, cleared the table, and carried the utensils, dishes and condiments into the kitchen, only occasionally bumping elbows or getting in each other's way. His thoughtfulness pleased her. She liked a man willing to pitch in and help, whether in business or domestic duties. Janey returned to shoo them out. "You two go back out on the patio and relax. Hugh and I will both be there in a second."

"Think that's a ploy to get us alone?" Ross asked as they settled into the cushioned redwood chairs. A soft cool breeze blew across the backyard. The sounds of the boys chasing fireflies rose, then became dim. The smell of honeysuckle and hyacinth permeated the air lulling Eileen into an even more genial mood.

"If so, you don't seem very annoyed," she commented softly.

Ross put his arms above his head and stretched contentedly. "I'm used to it." He grinned, cocking a speculative brow. "Unattached men are fair game for every matchmaker in the vicinity. I imagine widows are, too."

It was hard to stay piqued with him, no matter how much he'd meddled earlier, when he was in such a charming mood. She laughed. "I've learned to grin and bear it when unexpectedly partnered with a man, and to avoid blind dates like mad. Janey knows that, of course, which was the reason for the big surprise."

He shot her an interested glance. "How do you

find being a single parent?" There was a twinge of envy in his voice. Eileen remembered what Janey had said about Ross's son, Steve.

Eileen twined her hands together in her lap. "Tough but rewarding. At times it's a real juggling act. Sometimes it's pure pleasure. I wish Teddy'd been given the chance to know his father." When Ted, Sr., had been happy and complete, she added to herself.

Ross scrutinized her closely. "He doesn't have anyone to step into the role, even temporarily?" Teddy's loss seemed to matter to him. But it was more than the fact of shared experiences, that they both had been left to grow up without a father. It was fiercely personal. Because he had been unable to be with his own son while he was growing up.

"Only Hugh, and occasionally his grandparents." She sighed. She was just beginning to realize it wasn't enough, not for a growing boy in need of a role model. Teddy needed someone to share and explain the curious blows life dealt from a male point of view, on a day-to-day basis. He needed the devotion that only came from a permanent live-in father. And that was the one thing she could not provide.

Ross rose lithely from his chair. "Would you like to walk down to check on the boys?" The children were barely visible, playing recklessly and rowdily at the end of Janey's one-acre lot.

"Maybe we'd better." It was a tentative step toward friendship, and she flushed slightly at the husky catch in her voice. Ross offered her a hand up. He didn't let go of her, even after they started to walk. The clasp of his warm fingers on hers was oddly stirring, sensual. For the first time in an eternity she felt completely at ease with a man and at the same time breathlessly aware. A shiver made her tremble and, mistaking the involuntary movement for coldness, Ross moved closer, his grasp tightening. Suddenly she felt an urge to know more about him, about what prompted his intense interest in Teddy. "How long were you married?" In remarkably easy, fluid cadence they walked together over the grassy knoll.

"Seven years," he replied softly.

Her heart clenched at the revelation. That was a long time, nearly three and a half times the interlude she had spent with Ted.

"How long have you been divorced?" She stopped, swinging partway around to face him, all too aware of the thrumming of tension in her throat.

"Seven years." Ross sighed and glanced evasively up at the oaks and elms overhead. Wordlessly, they resumed walking. He clasped her hand more tightly, his dark gaze reassuring.

But her doubts persisted. Was he still in love with his wife? Had she left him, or had it been the other way around? He seemed to be too bitter about the experience for it not to have been traumatic. "Do you ever see your ex-wife?"

One corner of his mouth lifted in wry acknowledgment. "The last I heard Arielle was living in Europe and summering in Bermuda, although that could have changed on a whim." His voice was testy as he added, "She makes it a distinct point to keep in touch as seldom as possible."

"I'm sorry." Obviously, he'd been hurt by the breakup. Eileen wanted to soothe that pain.

"So was I, for a while." His tone was calm, his glance geared straight ahead. He seemed lost in thought.

"And now?" Anticipation tightened her muscles as she waited for his reply. *Please, don't let him still be carrying the torch*, she thought.

Both sides of his beautiful mouth lifted buoyantly. "I'm glad I'm free." He pivoted to face her, holding her forearms lightly in his hands. His eyes searched her face as she stared up at him in the shadows, heart pounding, confused by the powerful attraction she felt. It was happening too swiftly, and yet, considering all the years alone, not nearly fast enough. Part of her wanted this man in her life with something near desperation, and that scared her.

"What about you?" he asked softly, his touch hot and searing against her skin, yet at the same time gentle. "How do you feel about your former husband? Are you still in love with him after all these years? Is that why you keep yourself so aloof?"

The reasons for that she couldn't confide. Her throat was unbearably dry. "I—"

There was a strange glimmer in his eyes, an angry tautness on his face. "Was it a good marriage, one of those relationships made in heaven? Or was it less than perfect, perhaps even illusion-shattering?" When she didn't answer, he said, less impatiently, "I'm not wrong, am I? Your marriage hurt you, too. It just ended in a different way."

He was getting too close to the truth, evoking too many past hurts. Her spine stiffened and she glanced away. "I really should check on the boys."

For a second Ross held her motionless, refusing to let her slip away. Then, realizing the conversation really was over he let her go and started forward. "I'll come with you." When they reached a particularly rocky section of the yard, he slid a bracing arm about her waist. Despite her agitation, her response was swift and electric. At his nearness, her knees weakened. Her world narrowed until she could hear only the rise and fall of his breath, smell his aftershave, sense the bridled strength in his wiry arms and legs. Involuntarily, she imagined his kiss and wondered if he would use the same commanding touch in his lovemaking. The thought only aroused her more.

They reached the edge of the yard. Silvery streamers of moonlight spilled across the landscaped terrain. The Deverauxes' in-ground swimming pool glimmered darkly, dangerously between where she and Ross stood and where the boys played. Before she could voice a warning, Teddy started forward, heedlessly closing the thirty or so feet between them. "Hey, mom, watch this!" Teddy yelled absorbedly, still chasing a cluster of flashing yellow fireflies.

Automatically, Eileen started to warn him to be careful, to slow down, to watch what he was doing and where he was going. But she was too late. Teddy was already staggering across the pebble-strewn cement walkway to the darkness of the unlit pool. Eyes still on the firefly hovering just above his reach, Teddy made a final grab with his open fist. The recklessness in his movement sent him tumbling forward, then sideways as he fought to regain his balance. Eileen's heart stopped beating as his shoe caught on the edge of a nearby chair. He hurtled forward, hanging completely suspended for one clawing, clownish moment before plunging into the black depths of the Deverauxes' swimming pool. Recovering enough to draw a panic-stricken breath, Eileen screamed. Teddy didn't surface. Swiftly and without a sideward glance or pause, Ross shucked his shoes and dived fully clothed into the deep end after her son. Brian stood slack-mouthed, inert, the firefly he had captured escaping from his hand. Praying wordlessly, Eileen circled around to the edge of the pool where Teddy had fallen in, grabbing the life vest and white Styrofoam inner tube as she went.

Hugh, on his way out the back door of the house, saw what was happening and immediately ran to flick on the pool lights. A second later Teddy surfaced, near the shallow end, completely unharmed and grinning breathlessly. Ross followed, flinging the water from his hair. Teddy, laughing, excitedly yelled he was all right. "Hey, mom, you should see it down there at night!" he continued with a shuddering breath. "The water's all black and you can't tell which way is up or which way is down—"

Relieved and shaken, Eileen promptly burst into tears. "Teddy," she shouted emotionally. "You scared me to death!"

"Aw, mom, you know I can swim!" He pulled himself up over the side of the pool, grinning mischievously from ear to ear. Despite herself, she softened maternally at the sight of him safe and dripping.

"Well, I didn't," Ross Mitchell said wryly as he emerged dripping wet from the other end of the pool. Ross sloshed slowly toward her, rivulets of water following in his wake.

"Oh, Ross, I am so sorry!" she said. Still mesmerized by his disgruntled glare, she handed him a towel from a nearby chair and watched helplessly as he toweled his head and shoulders dry.

"Don't be." He grinned suddenly. "I always enjoy an evening swim."

Eileen glanced from one wet male to the other. Sure that Teddy was all right, she went to Ross's side and spoke in a low tone. "Thank you. I don't know what I would have done if.... Your quick thinking might have saved Teddy's life." She knew now why the boys looked up to him. Not only was he brave, but he had a sense of humor to get through the worst of times, too.

"You would have done the same if the situation were reversed," he said confidently. "And as for the stunt, such tomfoolery is par for the course in raising little boys." His soft tone let her know he understood and didn't stand in judgment of either Teddy's behavior or her parenting. Her respect for him increased.

Still, chagrin and embarrassment sent hot color seeping into her cheeks. "Well, thank you again."

"Anytime."

She returned her attention to her son. Chlorinated water streamed in rivulets from Teddy's dark green camp shorts and polo shirt. His shoes squished loudly with every step. Although apparently still very amused by the whole fiasco, Teddy's boyish glee faded as he took in her disapproving expression.

Hugh intervened calmly. "Brian, you take Teddy on up to the house and see he dries off and gets into some clean clothes of yours. Don't try and give him anything of the girls' to wear."

Trying not to giggle, they left. Eileen sighed, trembling with the thought of what might have been had Teddy not known how to swim. She turned as Ross approached her. If his masculinity had been potently obvious before when he was dressed in a neatly pressed business suit, it was now glaringly apparent as his thin cotton sport clothing wetly molded his lean form. He was all muscle, from the corded columns of his thighs and calves to his taut stomach and powerful chest. His hair was slicked darkly back away from his face. Water beaded his eyelashes and brows. Beside him, at five foot eleven, Hugh looked like a bespectacled elf.

Hugh shook his head. "Kids!"

Eileen had a few ideas about what she would say to her son when she got him alone. Hugh surveyed

Ross with amusement, then motioned to a small square building at the other end of the pool. "There are some more towels in the cabana, Ross."

Ross cast a speculative glance toward the house. "Do you think Janey would object if we tossed what I've got on now into her dryer?"

"No problem—I'll do it myself," Hugh assured.

Eileen, sensing her presence to be more of a hindrance than a help at that point, politely took off toward the house. "I'll see if I can get you a robe or something to wear in the meantime," she said. Janey was in the kitchen, and Eileen filled her sister in on the details of the incident, including her suspicion that Teddy had recklessly choreographed the whole spill in a bid for Ross's attention.

Janey frowned, leading the way upstairs toward Hugh's closet. "Well, you know Teddy does like the attention of the men. And Ross has demonstrated a genuine interest. Can you blame him for trying to take advantage of that interest?"

Eileen sighed, threading her fingers through her hair. "Believe me, I feel guilty enough already because I haven't provided him with a father."

"Then do something about it. Let Teddy play softball for Ross. He's a good man, Eileen—a wonderful role model, someone Teddy can admire, who'd be willing to give him the attention he needs. Hugh tries to fill in the gaps, you know, but we've got four kids of our own. And with Brian the only boy here, and sometimes left out, too, it's very difficult."

She was right, Eileen knew.

Janey pulled out a plush maroon terry-cloth robe. "No doubt Ross will fill this to overflowing, but at least it will be warmer than just a towel."

The pool area was illuminated only by the shimmering underwater lights, when Eileen approached several minutes later. Neither Ross nor Hugh was visible. "Hugh?" Eileen called softly, goose bumps forming on her arms, shoulders, the back of her neck. She'd never liked being alone at night in the dark, and the eeriness of the deserted yard with its abundance of heavily leafed trees frightened her.

"Over here," said a muffled male voice.

Shivers of awareness slid down her spine but she relaxed slightly, feeling immeasurably safer now that she knew he was in the vicinity. "Ross?" Her voice trembled slightly on the soft cool night air.

"In the cabana," he directed, his voice becoming clearer and more distinct as she neared the building.

"Where's Hugh?" She felt ridiculous talking to a building, but she was almost afraid to go any closer. What if there hadn't been any towels in there? Or worse, only ones that didn't quite fit? She didn't know if she wanted to see Ross Mitchell half naked, even for an instant. He was desirable enough as it was. Even now she couldn't get the image of him dripping wet in his clothes from her mind.

A low laugh rumbled on the other side of the cabana walls. "He took off with my clothes," Ross answered with dry reserve. "Naturally, I haven't seen him since."

His display of humor unnerved her further. Struggling to keep a grip on her composure, she said, "Oh. Well, I—I brought you a robe. I'll just...leave it here...."

The cabana door opened before she'd finished. Ross emerged with a relieved sigh, his movements languorously elegant. He was naked, except for the short terry-cloth towel around his waist. The fabric was old and faded, worn thin from too many washings. Eileen was dismayed to discover that it didn't quite reach completely around his waist, and where it gapped, a three-inch span of taut hip and thigh was exposed. Eileen swallowed, her throat suddenly unbearably dry. It had been years since she'd seen her husband completely unclothed, and she couldn't recall his ever looking quite that touchable or relaxed. Unable to take her eyes from Ross's rugged body, she stared speechlessly. Every inch of his corded legs was covered by sable-brown hair. His chest was luxuriantly furred, the coarse hair growing in an inviting T across the muscled plane, the compelling dark line disappearing into the waistline of the towel. Her face flushed when her gaze lowered and she realized just how much of his male silhouette was visible beneath the too-thin cloth. And, unless she was more off the mark than she thought, just as aroused as she.

Casually, Ross reached for the robe. "Thanks."

She jumped at the contact of his hand brushing hers and he smiled gently, his body stilling until he barely seemed to breathe.

The towel fell to Ross's feet. Nonchalantly, he shrugged into the robe, the light of the cabana illuminating him in all his natural glory.

Ross methodically belted the robe. If he was aware he'd shocked her speechless, he didn't show it. Switching off the cabana light, he shut the door, walked out toward the pool and sank into a chair. Her knees weak, Eileen did the same. She didn't think she could have walked ten feet at that moment if her life depended upon it.

"Boy, this feels good." Ross sighed, stretching his long legs out in front of him. His dark hair was still wet, curling haphazardly around his ears. The robe covered only half his muscular arms and just touched his knees, but at least it covered him completely at the waist, she noted with relief. "I was getting awfully tired of standing there in the dark," he finished with a beleaguered sigh.

"Would you like me to go and check on your clothes?" she asked, already rising halfway out of her chair. Her heart was pounding so loudly she could hear nothing else.

He glanced at his watch quickly. "I doubt they're dry yet. Give it another fifteen minutes or so." He looked at her, his brow furrowing. "Unless, of course, you're uncomfortable sitting here with me only in a robe."

Eileen was about to admit it when she caught the challenging glint in his eyes. Provoked, yet not wanting him to know just how disturbed she had really been, she sank lazily back into the webbing-covered chair with as much feigned indifference as she could muster. "Not at all." Two could play the game. Instinct told her he was as determined to win as she.

Silence stretched between them. Eileen glanced upward, noting the many stars sprinkling the dark-blue velvet sky. She relaxed slightly. No doubt Hugh or Janey or both would return momentarily. And if not them, then the boys. And then she could exit gracefully, take Teddy home.

"Teddy does swim well, doesn't he?" Ross's voice was as rich and smooth as aged brandy, and just as potent. Eileen smiled and nodded and again shifted restlessly in her chair, plucking at an imaginary thread on her jeans. Oh, for heaven's sake, this was getting ridiculous! She wished he would stop looking at her as if she were a pound of ultraexpensive chocolates just waiting to be consumed. She had to keep her mind on the conversation, not on what he did or didn't have on beneath the robe!

"I enrolled him in swimming classes from the

time he could walk," she informed, matching Ross's matter-of-fact tone. "Janey did the same for her children. In fact, Teddy and Brian took lessons together."

Ross nodded approvingly. "Well, next time I'll know better. I won't be quite so quick to dive in." He sent her a contemplative look that skimmed the flowing mass of her hair and softly parted lips. As if realizing how vulnerable he made her feel, his voice softened even more. "I wish you'd reconsider and bring Teddy to softball practice tomorrow morning. See for yourself whether you think it's a worthwhile endeavor or not."

She vacillated briefly, swayed by the sincerity of his words. "All right," she said finally. Perhaps it was time she faced the past, as well as did something about using up her son's store of excess energy. "But now if you'll excuse me, I really must be going." She couldn't sit there with him any longer. The experience was stirring up all sorts of hidden, secret impulses, making her remember how long it had been since she had made love with a man, been held, touched, caressed. And despite her attraction to Ross on both an emotional and physical level, she didn't take lovemaking or even the suggestion of it nearly as casually as he apparently did, if his near nudity and virile ease were any indication.

She stood, and Ross followed suit. "I'd offer to walk you to the house," he joked with a rakish lift of his brows.

"I think I can find it," she assured him tartly, glancing up at the house. No one was on the patio or in the yard, though the two-story home was lit as brightly as a Christmas tree. She hoped Teddy was dressed and ready to go. If Ross were to attempt to delay her . . . .

As if reading her thoughts, Ross gently touched her arm. She turned toward him, her mouth open with a half-formed question. He hesitated just a fraction of a moment, and then his head dipped toward hers. "Isn't it customary for the hero to receive a kiss?" he asked softly, his lips hovering just above her own. The warmth of his breath mingled with hers. "If not from Teddy, then perhaps his mother, the next most grateful person?" he teased.

What was meant to be a warning came out a whisper. "Ross!" she reprimanded breathlessly, but his hands were already sliding sensuously across her back.

"Don't talk," he murmured, his soft lips coming treacherously close. His warm, fragrant breath whispered across her face to her ear and then back across her cheek to her mouth. "Just kiss."

She had no more chance to protest. His mouth closed gently over hers. His other arm went around her waist, drawing her even nearer. Suddenly, she yearned to give him her affection, her thanks. Even more, she was eager to experience the unique magic of his caress. If she were honest, she knew she'd wanted it from the first instant he'd emerged from the pool. Everything that had gone on since had just been a waiting game, played out tentatively on both sides. The pressure of his mouth increased like a butterfly wedging entrance into her soul. Sensations, unbidden, only half-remembered, engulfed her, and she swayed against him, needing his strength, wanting his love. And then he was holding her possessively, cherishing her even as he desired her. Eileen's arms wreathed his neck, the tips of her fingers brushing against the lush dampness of his hair. Her breasts pushed toward the uncompromising plane of his chest, and then when he folded her more intimately against him, they yielded to the cool firm skin, her nipples flowering involuntarily beneath the constraint of her blouse and bra.

Sensing her acquiescence, Ross tenderly deepened the kiss, christening her into the smooth, slightly salty, masculine flavor of his skin, the seductive warmth of his parted lips. Testing, seeking, he coaxed her into further response and relished what he found. She was swept from gratitude to passion and then into a wellspring of desire. And still he wanted more of her. Using the flat of one palm he pressed her against him intimately, from shoulder blade to hip. His hard thighs molded to hers. The revelation of his sex was a throbbing, insistent ache, pressing ever closer, upward. She shifted away. He beguiled her back. The sensation of his hard length pressed so inexorably against her added fuel to the flame. His tongue gently nudged her teeth apart, and she responded ardently kiss for kiss, allowing him better, more intimate access to the honeyed cavern of her mouth. Their tongues met, twined. Her palms slid across the breadth of his shoulders, across his chest, collarbone, around the back of his neck to mesh in the curling damp strands that trailed lower into the neckline of his robe toward the base of his spine. He maneuvered her closer still, the dampness of his body through the robe making her aware of every sinew, every racing pulse beat of desire. His hand coasted over her ribs to rest just below her breast, waiting, as if seeking permission. He wanted her. She desired him. And yet there were so many reasons why they shouldn't be together like this, especially here at the Deverauxes' pool. Realizing what she was asking, inviting to happen, Eileen pulled away. He stared down into her face. "I won't apologize," he said softly as the seconds drew out.

"Because I've been wanting to do that from the moment I saw you."

Her breath was rising and falling rapidly in her chest. Feeling unbearably weak-kneed and vulnerable, Eileen put her hands up to both steady herself and ward him off. She had never been able to make love with a man casually. Yet her every instinct told her a love affair with Ross would never be unimportant. His steady, ardent look confirmed it. "I want to make love to you, Eileen." His hand made slow, lazy circles across her back.

She pulled away, annoyed with herself for letting him think her that accessible. "Ross, my son is just yards away."

"He's never seen you kiss a man?" Ross's voice was soft with disbelief. He waited, searching her face for reaction.

She flushed hotly. "I've only dated occasionally," she admitted finally. "More for friendship than anything else, and then only rarely. With my job and taking care of Teddy, I simply don't have the time."

He remained implacable. "Maybe you should make the time." She'd never wanted to before. "So you're telling me you've never been seriously involved with anyone other than your husband." He seemed to like the idea.

"No." She'd never even been tempted, until now.

"I see." Ross sighed, the tension easing from his body as he exhaled. He didn't step away from her, but neither did he try to touch her again. "Practice starts tomorrow at nine," he informed in cool, precise tones. "I'll look forward to seeing both you and Teddy then."

Hugh was already on his way down to the cabana, Ross's dried clothes in his hands. Wordlessly, Eileen turned and started for the house. She told herself she felt only relief—that the disappointment constricting her heart was not for the lovemaking that might have been.

3

"PROMISE ME YOU'LL BE on your best behavior this morning," Eileen urged early the next morning as Teddy finished the last of his apple-and-raisin oatmeal cereal. He was dressed in jeans, sneakers and an old but much-favored Cincinnati Reds T-shirt. He grinned at her alertly and ducked his head, his tousled blond hair falling across his brow, "Aw, mom—"

"I mean it, Teddy." She faced him, her expression deliberately severe. "No more showing off."

Hurriedly he drained the last of his milk, then wiped his mouth on his arm before she could admonish him. "I promise I'll be good. Is it okay if I brush my teeth before we go?"

What a clever way to cut the lecture short, she thought, but again her tone carried a faint warning note. "Of course." She didn't want any more instant replays of his dangerous tomfoolery of the evening before.

Relieved at her having cut short her admonition, Teddy raced for the stairs, his shirttail flapping out of the waistband of his pants. She watched him go, shaking her head. It was hard to believe anyone could be so exuberant at seven-thirty on a Saturday morning. Generally both of them slept late. But this morning her son had been up at the crack of dawn. She'd heard him running imaginary bases around the living room before she'd even lifted her head from the pillow, calling out the fictitious score and the action as he went. She hadn't realized he knew so much about baseball. Nor had she realized how much he wanted to play. Now, watching him volunteer to brush his teeth without being told, she knew baseball was first on his list of priorities, something she'd be heartless to deprive him of. And yet there loomed the threat that the more he learned about baseball, the more he'd undoubtedly want to know about his father. Unfortunately, not all of what he'd discover would make him proud. And she didn't want Teddy hurt, not like she'd been so long ago.

Teddy came tumbling back down the stairs at eight o'clock. "Ready to go?" he asked impatiently.

She smiled, reminding him, "Practice doesn't start until nine."

"It'll take us half an hour to get there."

Fifteen minutes, she thought. "I have to get dressed, but then I'll be ready to go. Don't worry. We won't be late."

"Okay, but don't take too long." Teddy settled himself on the sofa in front of the Saturday-morning cartoons. Eileen ruffled his hair affectionately then headed for the stairs. She dressed in triple-pleated khaki trousers and a gauzy white blouse, slid espadrilles over her bare feet and ran a brush through her hair. Finally, she applied a touch of lip gloss and blush. When she returned, Teddy was where she had left him. The scowl on his face told her he was well aware nearly half an hour had passed. "We won't be late," she assured patiently again.

"Hmph" was all he said.

Most of the other boys had arrived when they reached the ball park. After a moment's hesitation, Teddy ran over to join Ross. Eileen settled on the bleachers above the field. Except for one almost cursory glance Ross seemed completely oblivious to her presence. She told herself that was the way she wanted it, but as practice progressed, her mood sank lower. Ross was a gifted, fair, patient coach, that much was clear. The boys were devoted to him. And Teddy would do well under his tutelage, she knew. She was worried about herself now, and how she would deal with repeated contact with such a virile, attractive man. Even if nothing more passed between them, she'd still be recalling his kiss of the night before, the tenderness of his hands as they caressed her back from shoulder blade to hip, how fervently she'd returned his embrace before coming to her senses. . . .

"Okay, boys," Ross Mitchell was calling, jerking her from her thoughts. "That's about it for today! Run over to the concession stand. There's a glass of lemonade and a bag of popcorn for each of you, my treat!"

A cheer went up from the boys and they raced off obediently. Ross Mitchell's eyes found hers, held. Slowly, he started her way. He was dressed in an old hooded gray sweatshirt, short gray running shorts, knee-high athletic socks, and well-worn red-and-white Nikes. A whistle was on a string around his neck. He held a clipboard and pen in one hand. She stood as he approached, shading her eyes from the hot yellow glare of the sun with her right hand.

"Well, what'd you think?" He stopped just short of the bleachers, his feet apart and planted firmly in the grass. Despite herself Eileen was aware of every taut muscle, the not unpleasant sheen of perspiration beading his face. "Going to let Teddy join the team?"

She slowly threaded her way down, waiting until her feet touched the ground before she spoke.

"You'll take him this late in the season?" Her voice was soft and melodic when compared with the low, gravelly pitch of his.

White teeth gleamed in a devastating smile. "You bet!"

The man was a heartbreaker, Eileen thought. He ought to carry a sign warning vulnerable women to beware. "It seems to be what Teddy wants," she admitted after a moment, not quite stifling a reluctant sigh.

At her tone, he tensed momentarily, his gaze lazily taking in the results of her careful choice of clothes. He grinned down at her, towering over her physically. "You'll have to translate that look for me. Is that a yes or a no?"

His eyes said he wanted so much more than the rights to teach her son an athletic endeavor, but his tone was above reproach. "Yes." Her throat tightened as she gave her consent.

"Great!" Ross bent toward a stack of equipment. "I've got a uniform for him in the car."

Confident I'd agree, weren't you, she thought wryly, shaking her head.

He continued pleasantly, "It would help if he had some shoes with cleats on them for better traction, but frankly, ordinary tennis shoes will do." Ross turned toward her, his arms full of bats, gloves and catcher's equipment. "How about helping me cart some of this to my Jeep?"

Eileen picked up the remaining bats and gloves. "Sure." They walked toward the parking lot, the sun beating down hotly overhead. In the distance they could hear the boys yelling and laughing, but trees and bleachers shaded the concession stand from view. She tried not to notice the shirt stretching damply across his chest, the long muscled legs beneath the hem of his comfortably fitting shorts. To no avail. In her mind she was remembering the sight of him unclothed, the thin bath towel wrapped around his waist, dropping to the ground. How utterly magnificent he'd looked for the split second or two he'd remained unclothed!

As they reached the parking lot, Ross gave her a searching glance. "Look, if you're upset about what happened between us last night—" he began softly.

"I'm a grown woman, Ross. I can handle a kiss." Her tone was purposefully dry.

His mouth curled in disbelief. "Then why so quiet?"

How could she explain that just having him next to her, so close and so virile, made her tongue-tied and shy? That in just one twenty-four-hour period he made her see how hopelessly empty her life had been? Not as a mother—there she was fulfilled. But as a woman, a person, an adult in need of companionship. He'd made her yearn to be loved again, made her want the degree of satisfying intimacy obtained in a man-woman relationship. He'd made her feel impossibly young and yet so very old.

They arrived at a dusty, battered Jeep wagon. He circled around the back, flung open the tailgate and tossed the athletic equipment onto the floor. Wordlessly, she followed suit with the bats and gloves. He handed her the uniform for Teddy. His gaze trailed lazily over her and returned to her face, and again he favored her with that wonderful, engaging smile. Lifting his shoulders in a careless shrug, he ventured, "As long as you're not mad at me, how about a date? We could take in a movie, maybe have a late-night supper at my place. I'm a whiz when it comes to cooking steaks on the grill. I do a fair job on roast chicken, too." Reading her indecision, he added, "If you're worried about the cost of a sitter, I'll pay for that, too."

"It's not that," she hastened to explain. "I can handle the expense. I wouldn't need one anyway, tonight. Teddy's sleeping over at a classmate's. There's a birthday party camp-out in their backyard." Too late, she realized she'd told him too much. She swallowed and went on, telling him what had been bothering her. "What I am worried about is the fact that you're coaching Teddy now. I . . . wouldn't want any of the other children to resent him or me." She didn't want her son to be hurt. And if a friendship or romantic relationship did not evolve for her and Ross, it could later prove to be awkward.

"I don't think it will be a problem." He rubbed a hand along his jaw, as if unconsciously memorizing the angular masculine shape. "Have you made other plans?"

"No."

He slammed the tailgate shut and turned to face her. He paused contemplatively. "I don't want to rush you, Eileen. I do want you to think about it." His gaze touched on her from head to toe, as if preserving the memory of that day, that moment, for all time. "If you change your mind, I'll be at my law office the rest of the day."

To her chagrin he seemed fairly confident she would call. In the distance, the boys were scattering over the diamond. Silently, not touching, Eileen and Ross walked over to join them.

THE REST OF THE DAY PASSED dismally for Eileen. Several times she reached for the phone, intending to call Ross and tell him, yes, she would go. She always stopped just short of dialing as she recalled the easy way he had disrobed, her passionate reaction to his kiss. Just being with Ross would be treading on dangerous ground. Though tempted, she wasn't sure she was ready to complicate her life or her son's with the added scheduling difficulties and demands of a love affair. If Ross really did want to get to know her, he wouldn't mind waiting for her. If it was just an infatuation on her part, a physical reaction intensified from her years of being too long alone, the intense feelings of ardor whirling inside her would pass. Certainly, there was no reason for her to make a fool of herself or act like a teenager, both of which she was extremely tempted to do whenever in breathing distance of him. In the meantime, she'd stay away from him, see him only in relationship to the softball team and then only with other parents around.

At six o'clock she dropped Teddy off at his friend's house, sleeping bag, birthday present and suitcase in hand, and then returned to her town house. Alone for the first time in several weeks, she took a long bubble bath, smoothed on perfumed lotion and slipped into a silky floor-length raspberry print dress. The oval neckline dipped low across her breasts, softly molding to her damp skin. Twin spaghetti ties adorned each bare suntanned shoulder. She wore only a pair of bikini panties underneath.

Intent on enjoying her evening alone, she turned soft music on the stereo, fixed a cold supper and poured herself a glass of wine. After carrying a tray into the living room, she went to the bookshelves for a novel she was halfway through. Unhappily, the saga of three wealthy women paled in comparison to her own semitragic life. Her gaze caught on the long-abandoned photograph album, hidden halfway beneath a stack of year-old magazines. How long had it been since she'd perused those pages, she wondered, moving toward it. Would her frame of mind be less guilty if she allowed herself to remember, to grieve? She took the album back with her to the living-room sofa and curled up beside the lone shining lamp. Lost in the memories, the pictures of a much younger Eileen and Ted, Sr., she drifted until the doorbell rang, jarring her from her thoughts.

Wiping a tear from her cheek, she moved to the door. A peek through the one-way viewer alerted her to an impeccably groomed Ross Mitchell on her doorstep outside. She hesitated only briefly before opening the door.

They faced each other cautiously. He was wearing gray dress slacks and a tieless starched blue-gray-and-white tattersal shirt. His hair was neatly combed, his chin freshly shaven. Her heart pounded at his proximity, the drift of his after-shave, the way his eyes roamed her, as if savoring every inch. "Hi." He smiled again, and the gesture was as gentle as his voice. "I hope I'm not disturbing you, but I did want to bring these by."

For the first time she noticed the sheaf of papers in his left hand. He held it up before him like a shield. "I remembered a little while ago I forgot to give you the schedule of games for the rest of the season. I'm also going to need you to sign a release form, permitting Teddy to play in the league."

"Of course." She moved aside to let him in.

Ross glanced at the darkened living room, the throw pillows scattered across the sofa, the tray of fruit, crusty French bread, and cheese. "If you're expecting someone else, I could come back at another time."

"I'm not expecting anyone else, Ross—just indulging in a rare moment alone." She kept her voice light as she stooped to flick on another lamp. Nervously, she faced him, drawing on every bit of cordiality she possessed. "Would you care for a glass of wine?"

"I'd love one if it's not too much trouble."

When she returned, he was seated comfortably in an armchair. She handed him the glass of chilled Chardonnay, then sat down on the sofa, acutely aware of the inviting way she was dressed. Did he notice that her freshly washed hair, floating silkily over her shoulders, was still slightly damp and curling softly? Or that her face still carried the blush of the morning sunshine?

All business, Ross handed her the papers. "If there's anything you don't understand, just ask. I'll be glad to explain it." He leaned forward, pointing out the blank space near the bottom of the page. "I only need your signature on this last one."

"Fine." She swallowed tremulously as his hand brushed hers and then moved away. With difficulty, she forced her attention to the release, read it carefully, then signed it with a flourish. When she looked up, Ross was leaning forward slightly in his chair, his hands clasped between his knees. He was unabashedly studying the open pages of the album she'd left on the coffee table. "This your husband?" he asked softly.

"Yes." Eileen wished desperately she could thrust the memento of her marriage back into its dusty place.

"Is he the reason you don't date?" Ross asked curiously. "I asked you last night and you didn't answer me. Are you still in love with him, still bound to him in some way—through your son perhaps? I know through my law practice that some women are never able to consider remarrying or getting involved with another man again. But usually those women were married for twenty or thirty years or more."

Eileen sighed, handing him the platter of fruit and cheese. "The reason I don't date is that I work full-time days and take care of Teddy as well as everything else that has to be done weekends and evenings. As for Ted, Sr...." She sighed, looking down at her hands, the place where her wedding and engagement rings had been. "We were married so young and were together for so short a time, we never had a chance to build a real marriage."

Ross munched on a frosty green grape. "How did you meet?"

She smiled, recalling easily, "In college. We were both students at Purdue. I was a freshman and Ted was a junior. He was named All-American that year, and the pros were scouting. They offered him a contract to play baseball with the Cincinnati Reds." She lifted her glass and took another sip of wine. "Ted was in such a rush to get on with his life, to get out in the real world. He wanted to get married, have a child and be a professional baseball player all at once. He was a very dynamic person when everything was going his way. His enthusiasm was contagious, so with dreams of wealth and glory we both dropped out of college."

"What about your parents? How did they feel?"

"They disapproved heartily, but came around once we'd eloped and our union was a fact."

He grinned, as if empathizing with her story. "Are you close to them now?"

"Yes, I am, although I don't see them as often as I'd like. I try to drive up to their farm once every month or two. They live in northern Indiana. And of course Teddy stays there briefly every summer, as do Janey's children."

"Sounds like your parents are pretty terrific," he commented.

Ted never felt that way, Eileen thought. In fact he'd never really forgiven them for withholding their blessing. And then later when Ted's and Eileen's lives had turned sour, full of disappointments, he hadn't wanted to or been able to face her parents. Only after his death did her relationship with her family return to normal.

Unwilling to comment further, she flipped a page idly, the album opening to portraits of them together outside the justice of the peace sign. Ted was wearing a baseball uniform; she wore a girlish white-lace dress. How young she had been, Eileen mused. "How long were you married?" Ross asked, still studying her curiously.

"Almost three years."

"Were you happy with him?" Ross asked, swilling the last of the wine in his glass around and around.

"Yes." At least in the beginning. Later had been a different story, but she didn't want to get into that. The memories of that time still made her feel bitter. She flipped the album shut and pushed it aside. He was watching her steadily, as if he somehow knew she was telling him less than the whole truth. His intuitiveness made her nervous. "Can I offer you some more Chardonnay?"

"Please."

She refilled his glass, then hers. Studying each other covertly, they sipped their drinks. His glance dropped over the silk of her gown, lingered on her breasts, their rise and fall with every breath, before moving back to her face. She was so aware of him she could barely think, much less converse coherently, yet she knew she had to at least try to be normally at ease. "What about you? I know you're divorced. You intimated it was an unhappy experience. You didn't say how you felt about living alone again. Do you ever miss being married, sharing your life day to day with a woman, someone who cares?"

He rose and strolled restlessly over to examine a painting on the wall. His face was serious as he turned back to look at her. "I've learned to live one day at a time." He came back and took a seat on the sofa beside her.

"You're not seeing anyone steadily?" she asked, disturbed by the new huskiness of her voice. The more she was around him, the more drawn to him she was.

His hand had captured hers and was lightly infusing her with warmth. "No." He lifted her captured palm to his mouth, pressed his lips gently against it, then took the tip of her index finger into the liquid softness of his mouth. The sensation was as intoxicating as the man. "Ross—" she cautioned, feeling her bones melt slowly into mush. She didn't think she could stand up now if the house were on fire.

"I thought about you all afternoon," he confessed raggedly, prying the wineglass from her hands, then turning her so they were facing each other. "If I hadn't had a reason for stopping by tonight, I might have invented one."

His confession stole air from her lungs. "Why?" She moved over slightly, wedging a space between them with her bent, silk-clad knee.

The palms of his hands slid slowly up the length of her bare arms to her shoulders. He cupped the silky hair against her neck, crushing it with his hands, weaving his fingers through the bath-dampened strands. "I kept hoping you'd call me and say you'd changed your mind about seeing me tonight," he confessed. "I kept waiting for that phone to ring." His thumb moved up to trace the outline of her lips.

She trembled beneath the deliberateness of his caress, meant to draw away, and couldn't.

"I wasn't even sure you'd let me in tonight," he continued. "I wasn't sure you would really be alone." His other hand slid down her back, in sensual circular motions. Everywhere he touched, she was on fire, burning with desire.

Eileen drew back. He moved with her, his lips trailing down the side of her neck. She placed both hands on his shoulders, intending to hold him at bay briefly. Instead, she seemed to be clasping him to her, prolonging the contact, inviting even further advances. Emotion choked her throat, but she struggled to protest. "Ross, I don't want to lead you on." She didn't want to start something in her heart she knew she would be unable to finish.

He smiled down at her, as if her compunction only endeared her to him further. "I'm not asking you to make love to me, Eileen," he reassured her softly, "only to kiss me."

Could she trust herself to stop there, knowing how dizzy and desirous she was already feeling? "Ross, I—"

His mouth cut off her breathless disclaimer. She braced herself, but the kiss was sweet and gentle and tenderly compelling, and it sent the last of her objections spiraling away into nothingness. Sensing her surrender to at least his kisses, he eased her back onto the pillows. His warm chest covered hers, and his free hand wound in the silk of her hair. "You smell so good," he murmured, "like flowers blooming on a summer's day."

"It's my perfume."

He shook his head wordlessly. "No, it's the scent

of your skin and your hair. Beyond comparison. Like you."

And like him, she thought. Never had she met anyone who made her feel so special, who attracted her in the same mesmerizing way. Being with Ross was like being caught up in the eye of a hurricane, filled with halcyon calm, knowing there was no escape. His weight across hers made her feel protected, yet threatened, cosseted with love. Her heart pulsed erratically. She felt wild joy and disquiet and yes, even apprehension. She was beginning to want this and to want Ross entirely too much.

He watched her guardedly, momentarily halting the seduction, yet not about to give up what territory he had gained.

"I don't want to be hurt," she whispered, loathing the admission.

"I don't want to hurt you," he stated with quiet emphasis. "But I won't lie and say I don't want to make love to you, either, Eileen, because I do."

Heaven help her, she felt the same desire. "I do want to kiss you again." Her honesty shocked her and pleased him.

"Then just kissing it is." Slowly, by degrees, he lowered his mouth until their lips touched. Her lips parted under the pressure of his tongue, and he plundered the soft cavern over and over, seducing her into the maelstrom of his passion until she was gasping for breath, returning his caresses, teasing, evoking. With a groan he responded, drawing her even nearer. Her hands slid across his shoulders to his back. His mouth trailed kisses across her shoulder. Playfully, he caught the thin shoulder strap, holding her gown with his teeth. Before she could protest, the fabric was slowly drawn down across her left arm, revealing the uppermost curve of her breast. A sudden warmth flowed through her veins, as if she had just imbibed strong Irish whiskey. He seemed to be waiting for her to call a halt and when she didn't, his tongue skimmed lightly across her alabaster skin, sending another swift lightning bolt of desire through her. Her hips arched urgently.

"Eileen," he whispered, molding her to his prone length. And then there was nothing for her but that moment in time, the feeling of freedom. Freedom from her memories, the demands of her young son. In that moment she felt a girl again, on the brink of discovering love.

Her heart was beating so fiercely she thought he could hear it, but her body was already surrendering, bowing to needs and emotions gone unslaked. It felt so good to be held by him, she thought, so right. His mouth moved over hers, robbing her of breath, the need, the will to think. His palm coaxed the other strap down, pushed the fabric lower until both pink nipples were revealed. Chill air assaulted her skin as the tenderness of his hands warmed her soft breasts. "You're beautiful," he whispered, stroking with feather-light touches from their oval bases to cresting tips.

She moaned, feeling the rapid shuddering beat of his heart. "So are you." When he touched the tip of his tongue to her breast, she trembled. And then again, as his ministrations continued. "Ross—" Much more, and she really wouldn't be able to stop.

"Unbutton my shirt," he urged hoarsely. "Let me feel you against me."

Drugged with desire and the tenderness of his caress, she lifted her hand to the second button on his shirt. It came apart easily. Her fingertips slid inside to cherish the hair-whorled plane, teased downward to the next fastening, then withdrew. He groaned as if in mock pain, chiding her slowness, but she wouldn't be rushed, carefully working free the next button and the next, her eyes never leaving the compelling intensity of his. When she reached the barrier of his waistband, she parted the edges of cloth. Her palms slid outward just before he captured her mouth. She could taste the wine on both their breaths, mingling with the sweeter taste of the fruit, feel the warmth of his plundering tongue. But it wasn't enough for the woman within her and she arched against him wantonly, needing so much more than this, and yet afraid, unwilling to give more.

The sensation of his chest against hers was exquisite, overpowering, like being buried in the luxuriant softness of silky mink. They moved together faster, more urgently, his hands sliding beneath her to cup her hips. But when his hand reached for the hem of her skirt sanity returned. Eileen wasn't protected from pregnancy. No matter what their lovemaking might mean to her, or how much pleasure or comfort it might bring, it would still be little more than a one-night stand in reality. And for her to risk having another child, this one out of wedlock....

"No." She broke free and pushed away, adjusting the bodice of her dress back up over her breasts. "Ross, I can't." When he seemed to demand an explanation, she said, "I—I don't even know you, for heaven's sake!"

He sat up more slowly, pulling the edges of his shirt together. His cheeks were stained with the heat of his desire, his expression first frustrated, then accepting. "How much more do we have to know?" he asked quietly after a moment. "You want me. I want you. We're both adults. Not bound to anyone else in any way."

Shaken, she pushed the curtain of hair from her face. "It would still be wrong—for me."

He accepted her answer, honestly given. His anger faded, to be replaced by a tenderness oh so compelling. "Because we're not married?"

She lifted her eyes to his. "For me, making love is a commitment, ideally both an emotional and physical one. I'm not sure I would need to be married, although I was before, but I can't treat it lightly." She needed fidelity. She needed love, first and forever. She needed to understand herself and her reaction to Ross. Never had she been swept away like that, not even with her husband, either before or after they'd been married. What was different about Ross? What drew her to him so?

Ross sighed deeply. He rose, buttoning his shirt. "Believe it or not there was a time long ago when I felt that way, too." For a moment he seemed very sad, very far away.

"You're not angry?" That, she didn't want.

He grinned ruefully. "I promised to limit our tryst to just kissing." His mouth twisted in a wry grimace. "I didn't do that. Technically speaking, then, I think I got precisely what I deserved." His wit broke the tension between them. Blushing, she laughed softly, and he continued more seriously, "You're a lovely woman, Eileen. But this wasn't why I came over to see you tonight, or even why I stayed after the papers were signed."

She knew by his tone he was serious. She straightened apprehensively. "Then why?" What could be making him look so solemn?

"It has to do with Ted, Sr." He paused as her nerves constricted tightly. When she couldn't manage the last remaining shoulder tie of her dress, he came over and wordlessly helped her. "I learned the truth about your husband this afternoon, Eileen," he said quietly, stepping back. "And frankly, I think Teddy should be told."

4

"I KNOW TED HAD A DRINKING PROBLEM," Ross continued as she got slowly to her feet. He halted her instinctive denial with both palms upraised. "I know how he died, Eileen, so it's pointless to pretend the two of you had an idyllic life." Ross continued to survey her guardedly as he buttoned the throat of his shirt. "What I don't know is why you stayed with him as long as you did, or why, even now, you continue to cover up for a man who couldn't possibly have done much to inspire your devotion." He spoke with such distaste Eileen had to explain.

"It was more than a simple drinking problem that ruined Ted's life," she said quietly. "He was well on his way to becoming a full-fledged alcoholic." He'd also been drunk at the time he died, the alcohol level in his bloodstream well past the legal limit. If only the hurt had stopped there, she thought wistfully. If only the tragic results of his sickness had been limited to himself.

"Was that why he was dropped from the Majors?" Ross asked. He strode over to retrieve his glass. Bending, he poured himself more Chardonnay, then offered her a refill. She declined.

Eileen sighed. Her forearms hugged tight against her waist, she paced the room all too aware of his steady gaze following her. Her voice shook slightly as she spoke. "Ted was fond of saying that men who worked hard played hard. And he considered himself no exception to the rule. He liked to drink, period. In college he drank to celebrate and drank even more to console himself when his team lost, which was rarely."

"You say that as if you understand," Ross observed softly.

"I've accepted what happened." Eileen met his gaze, but couldn't sustain his intense scrutiny. She reached down to straighten a stack of magazines that didn't need rearranging. "Sometimes I think if he'd mastered the Major Leagues, he'd be alive now." Her fingertips slid over the glossy covers. "Other times, I don't know." She sighed. "Ted's whole life was baseball. It was his passion. I was a dim second place. Sometimes I can foresee the same sports obsession getting hold of Teddy. That's why his fierce desire to play upsets me so." She turned to face Ross. His silence made the confession easier.

"Ted spent three months in the Major Leagues. During that time, he was amazed at the free equipment and generous meal allowance he received. He loved the travel and the adoring fans and the celebrity status. True, he didn't play much, but just to be a part of it was thrilling to him. Unhappily, a technicality in his contract left him a free agent at the end of the first year. He was certain he would get all sorts of great offers—after all he was only twenty-one, he was talented, and in his first season with the Reds he'd done well. But he didn't get another offer. Instead, the team owner and manager felt he needed more seasoning, and they sent him to the Minor Leagues, to play on the Cincinnati farm team. It was a big step down. Ted no longer received much attention from either press or fans. His salary was substantially less. Still, Ted went after it with all his soul, batting a solid .280 during the first year, and a

respectable .275 the next. He was named to both the
International League and the Triple-A all-star teams.
And again, it didn't help. That winter, he worked at
a warehouse unloading trucks. By spring, he'd received no new offers. He knew he was destined for
another year on the farm team. To be truthful, it
didn't look as if he would ever make it to the Majors
again, at least not in the superstar way he had once
expected and still wanted. So Ted began drinking, at
first just on his days off, after games and sometimes,
rarely, before he played. Eventually, of course, he
got caught. The coach could have let him off with a
warning or a fine, if he'd been so inclined. He could
have sent him for counseling. Ted's record was
otherwise very good. But the political climate was
not conducive to cover-ups of any kind, and the
team fired him on a morals clause. It was about that
time I discovered I was pregnant. Ted was in no
shape to be a father. And he was, by that time, even
less of a husband to me, though he stubbornly refused to let me take over the family finances or manage even the simplest details of our lives. No, he
wanted to be the boss, and in retrospect I guess I
desperately needed someone to play the role of
white knight and whisk me away from all my problems. Sadly, it didn't work that way, though. Ted's
solution for our financial dilemma was for me to
have an abortion. He wanted to wait before starting
a family. But I wouldn't and couldn't destroy the
child we'd already made. So in retribution he began
hitting the bars, staying out all hours of the night,
coming home very drunk. Apologetic, of course, but
drunk. I knew most of his behavior was due to the
alcohol. I tried every tactic I knew to help him or to
get him to seek help himself. But he felt he was

washed up, that his life was over." Her mouth twisted ruefully.

"They say people with drinking problems have to first hit rock bottom before they will wake up to their problems and seek help. Ted was almost there when he died. He had been drinking heavily before that fatal car accident. Evidently he fell asleep at the wheel. A passing motorist found his car wrapped around a tree. The story was in all the papers. Reporters hounded me for weeks afterward, wanting to know more about Ted's mental state prior to his death. I refused to talk to them. Eventually they gave up."

"Why did you stay with him?" Ross asked gently. "Why didn't you leave him?"

"I probably would have, had the situation continued. But I kept hoping Ted would grow up, accept the responsibility of his child and find joy in the baby's arrival. And then, too, I wanted to help Ted. I hadn't married him just for the good times. I'd married him for better or worse and I hoped that once he recovered from his disappointment, he would go on to take charge of his life. I wanted him to be a success, and as my parents had disapproved of the match from the beginning, I needed to prove something to them too."

Ross was watching her with a new respect. "You're one hell of a woman to have put up with all that." Compassion for what she'd been through gentled the lines of his face.

"Or a fool." She'd been called the latter many times.

"I admire someone who stands by her commitments," he said softly, watching her with compassion.

Relief flooded her. She hadn't meant to tell Ross so much, but once started the words had had a momentum of their own. And now Ross knew. She wouldn't have to go on hiding.

"Teddy doesn't know any of this?" Ross set down his glass after a moment and came to her side.

"No." Briefly she leaned into the bracing arm he wrapped around her waist. "I've told him, of course, that his father played briefly for the Reds and then, in order to gain more experience, the farm teams."

Ross withdrew. "But not about the accident?"

She shook her head, weariness washing over her. "Nor being fired." She turned to Ross beseechingly. "Ted left him so little, I just can't bring myself to tell him his father was drunk at the time of his death."

Ross's mouth tightened with disapproval — whether at her actions or Ted's unsavory past, she didn't know. "He'll find out eventually, whether you want him to or not."

Eileen moved about the room, tidying up, plumping the pillows on the sofa. She knew Ross was right. Teddy was inherently curious. "When he's old enough to understand, I'll tell him." Her voice was low, her throat thick with tears. "How did you find out about Ted? Who told you?"

"One of the other coaches, who's an expert on baseball trivia. I mentioned I'd signed your son. He put the facts together. I researched the rest." He jammed both hands in his pockets. "The point is, Eileen, there are other people in the area who know. I think you should tell Teddy the truth, or at least pave the way, so that if it does come to that, he won't be so shocked. Or hurt."

"There's no way I could put any of this to him without destroying him," Eileen said softly. Ross couldn't disagree. Teddy was vulnerable, and other children and sometimes even parents were cruel. She sighed heavily, threading her fingers through her hair. "Now you know why I didn't want him to play in the first place."

"Eileen—" He started toward her, one hand outstretched imploringly.

"Ross, please, it's been a long evening." Sidestepping his approach, she led the way to the door. She needed time to collect her thoughts before Teddy came home.

"I'll call you in the morning." He hovered near the threshold, picked up the release form for Teddy and stood, reluctant to depart.

She felt as if they were back to square one, boxers facing off in the ring. "I'd rather you didn't," she said softly, "not until I work this dilemma out."

"I could help."

His offer was tempting, but she knew it was a problem only she could solve. "No, Ross, but thanks. I'll find a way to handle it." She clasped her arms beneath her breasts. "I appreciate your bringing it to my attention."

He nodded, taut with the reservations he was feeling. "If you need any help—"

"I'll call," she promised. But even as she spoke they both knew she wouldn't. He made no comment as he stepped out onto the walk and headed toward the curb, leaving her alone to solve the problem of Teddy.

TEDDY CAME BACK from his camp-out grubby and exhausted. Eileen sent him upstairs for a shower and some clean clothes, and after fixing him a light lunch, left him to enjoy a monster movie on TV. He slept most of the afternoon on the living-room sofa. Over dinner, she suggested, "Teddy, remember that camp we talked about earlier in the spring?"

His gaze was instantly alert, his expression happy. "Eagle Village?"

"Right, the one with the horseback riding and the swimming and arts and crafts."

He tilted his head, perplexed. "I thought you said it was too expensive."

"Well, I've been thinking about it, honey, and maybe we could get a loan, just for this year."

"But it's already started, hasn't it?"

"Yes, but I called and talked to the director today. She said they did have several openings from children who had moved. She said we could enroll you right away. In fact, you could go both sessions if you like."

"All summer?" He was overjoyed. After learning about the camp from one of his friends, he had bugged her incessantly for weeks.

Eileen sat back with a sigh. "If you like."

Abruptly, Teddy frowned, remembering. "What about Little League?"

"They have softball at camp, too."

He looked torn. "But it's not the same as playing in the league." He shrugged and stood, carrying his plate and silverware to the counter next to the sink. "Oh well, maybe next year."

"Don't you at least want to look at the camp, drive out and have a look around?" Eileen looked at him, astonished. She had been so sure this would work, without Teddy ever having to know how very much she didn't want him to play in the league.

"Nope, but thanks anyway, mom." He leaned over and planted a kiss on the top of her head. Hands stuffed into his pockets, he headed for the back door and the corner of the kitchen where he'd haphazardly stowed both his bat and his glove. "I think I'll go outside and practice my swings."

She sat there, dismayed. "You do that," she murmured idly, running a hand across the back of her neck. What was she going to do now?

Ross called later that evening, when Teddy was in bed. "Hi. How's it going with Teddy?" His low voice rumbled over the lines.

"He had a good time at his sleep-over."

"I'm glad." There was a silence. Ross cleared his throat. "Have you talked to him?"

"No. We did briefly discuss his attending camp this summer. He'd rather play on your team."

"I see." Ross sighed audibly. She could picture him raking a hand through his hair. "I want to see you again, Eileen. We need to talk. Lunch tomorrow?"

"I can't—"

"It's about Teddy."

All the more reason not to. Ross was too involved as it was. This was her problem to solve—she had to remember that. "I can't, Ross. But thank you for the invitation."

"There's no changing your mind?"

"No, I'm afraid not," she said quietly.

"Will you let him continue to play on the team?"

"For continuity's sake, I have to." But her tone made it clear it wasn't the route she would have chosen.

"I'm sorry you feel that way," he said, somewhat impatiently. "I had hoped to—" He stopped abruptly. "We still need to talk, and I'd rather do it face-to-face, preferably at an hour that won't cut into your time with Teddy. I'll meet you at noon tomorrow, Eileen. The bank lobby."

"Ross, no—" she said, but too late, he'd already hung up. Eileen stared at the receiver in amazement, then just as swiftly decided not to go. No man was going to arbitrarily tell her what to do—she didn't care what his motives were. Ross called several times the next morning, presumably to confirm their date. Eileen instructed her secretary to say she was busy, could not meet him and would instead call him sometime later in the week. Truthfully, the loan applications were piled up from a weekend of successful real-estate sales, and she was still working absorbedly at noon when Ross Mitchell appeared at her desk. She faced him reluctantly, a mixture of pleasure and exasperation on her face.

Ross was wearing his I-want-to-help-if-only-you'll-let-me look. Worse, everyone at the bank was no doubt remembering his insistence the last time he had visited her there.

"I don't have time to talk to you right now," she said softly.

"All business today, hmm?" His brows arched. There was a faintly mocking glitter in his eyes that made her flush.

She watched as he approached with an economy of motion, his jaw taut with suppressed impatience. "Yes."

"That suits me just fine. I'm here to apply for a loan." Before she could protest, he'd pulled up a chair in front of the desk. Aware of her open office door and the bank manager's eyes upon her, Eileen had no choice but to go through with the charade. Clients of Ross's financial stature were not rejected on a whim. Still, she bristled at his audacity, resenting his high-handed way of bringing personal matters to her attention on what should strictly have been the bank's time.

"Is it to be a personal or business loan?" Eileen sorted through the multicolored application forms. She stacked the forms efficiently on her desk.

He grinned in exaggerated patience. Crossing one

ankle across the opposite knee, he looped both hands casually around the bent leg. His eyes never left her face. "Personal."

It was getting harder to maintain an aloof demeanor. Eileen searched through her drawer for a pen. Wordlessly, he leaned forward and handed her a black ballpoint from beneath a stack of half-processed forms. His hand brushed hers inadvertently, sending a rush of warmth spinning through her. She wet suddenly dry lips, and without looking up knew he had followed the involuntary movement. She focused on the forms in front of her, but the print made no sense at all. Instead, she was thinking of his kiss, the way he had undressed her tenderly, dropping tiny kisses across the upper curves of her breasts. "I'll need detailed financial information."

He shrugged uncaringly at her request for pertinent information. Eileen groaned inwardly. She didn't want to know how much money he made, though judging from the quality of his suits and car, it was a substantial amount. She met his glance levelly. "Perhaps it'd be better if I got another loan officer to help you," she suggested firmly.

His brows drew together as if he were greatly perplexed. "Aren't you the senior loan officer here at the bank?" His tone was remarkably innocent. Obviously after the trouble she had caused him he was enjoying the hoax immensely.

The bank manager hovered near the door. He seemed to sense Ross was giving her trouble. Eileen forced a smile and waved her boss away, while at the same time answering Ross's question. "Well, yes," she hedged coolly. "But—"

Ross lifted both palms genially. "Then you're the one I want to do business with."

She sighed and leaned forward, resting one forearm on the desk. Maybe it would be better to just get it over with and get him out of there. "How much money were you thinking of borrowing, Mr. Mitchell?"

He lifted an imaginary speck of lint from his trousers. "Two hundred dollars."

Exasperation swept through her. It was all she could do to stifle a heavy sigh. Judging by the look on his face, he knew how much red tape the loan process required. He wasn't averse to putting her through it on a whim. "May I ask what for?" She put her pen down and rested both elbows on her desk, her hands clasped under her chin.

He looked at her directly for a breath-robbing moment, then flexed both shoulders, sighed, and rubbed at the back of his neck. "Does it matter?"

Her teeth clenched in aggravation behind the polite smile. The fact that she probably half deserved such an outlandish maneuver was of no consolation. "I need to put something on the application," she pointed out testily.

He shrugged again, his smile both wickedly challenging and disarming. Again she was reminded of his kiss, the way he had nonchalantly dropped his towel. How had she ever thought he would be an easy man to dismiss? "I really didn't have any special purpose in mind. I did have this lunch date, though. An important one, to my way of thinking." The message seemed clear. She wasn't to avoid his calls again. If she didn't want to see him, he wanted to hear her say it personally, with no lies and no evasions.

Eileen held his steady stare. Knowing as she did the gallant motivations behind his actions, it was getting more difficult to remain angry with him. Commanding herself to attention, she sat straighter. "Then why are you borrowing the money?"

His eyes met hers straight on. Again, she could imagine herself getting lost in the turquoise depths. "Because I wanted to see you, and I figured this was the only way."

"I told you. I'm busy."

"So am I, Ms Garrett, so am I." He'd made his point.

"I don't take personal calls during working hours."

"Which is precisely why I brought my business to you. If this is indeed the *only* way we can talk...." He left the thought unfinished.

Irritated, she ran a hand through her hair, brushing the bangs to the side. "Mr. Mitchell—"

"Ross," he corrected, eyeing her intently. All too aware of the open office door, he leaned forward, both hands still casually clasping his bent knee. "I'll ask you one more time, Eileen. Have lunch with me."

She swallowed hard. Reading her near surrender, he promised softly with a rakish grin, "I'll cease and desist bothering you here at work if you do."

That part of the offer was tempting. He stood nonchalantly, thrusting his hands into his pockets. "I don't want you mad at me. It's bad for my image."

Image of what, she wondered. "Womanizer or coach?" She hadn't meant to say the words aloud.

Amusement curved the corners of his mouth. "Both," he assured.

Oh, dear, Eileen thought. She had been fantasizing about him all the previous day. Still, she couldn't let him think he could push her around. "You promise you'll never bother me here again if I go with you?"

"Absolutely." About that much he was serious. He crossed his heart. "On my word of honor as a gentleman."

Eileen rummaged in her desk drawer for her

purse. Part of her said she was a fool for going, but the romantic side of her was relieved. Despite everything, she had wanted to see Ross again. And maybe he could help her solve her problem. Janey said he had raised a son, too. "I've only got an hour," she cautioned, reaching for the jacket draped over the back of her chair. Gallantly, he helped her shrug into it.

"Unless I've lost my touch, that's all I'll need."

THEY DINED AT A LOCAL BUFFET. Ross ate like an athlete in training, heaping his plate with hearty slices of roast beef, au gratin potatoes and an assortment of hot and cold vegetables. Conscious of her weight, Eileen contented herself with a large iced tea and a lightly dressed chef's salad.

Silence stretched between them. She knew there was so much he didn't understand. Suddenly, perhaps because he had been so concerned, she wanted to confide in him further. "You think I'm being unreasonable because, in my heart, I still really don't want Teddy to play ball."

He lifted his shoulders in a careless shrug, but his eyes were penetratingly alert. "It is your decision, but yes, I have wondered if there isn't more than what you've already told me."

Aware that Ross was waiting for her to continue, she said, "Baseball was an obsession with Teddy's father. He had stories of practicing day and night when he was only four or five years old. According to Ted, Sr., you could no more have stopped him from doing that than you could have stopped Mozart from dreaming up music or van Gogh from painting. I believed him. You see, for Ted, baseball had been the only way out of an impoverished background, and he was determined to succeed, come hell or high water. Up until the time we met and even afterward, it symbolized everything meaningful and hopeful to him in life. And when it didn't work out, he wasn't able to cope, at least not right away." They'd never had the chance to find out if Ted would have pulled himself together with the grit and sheer determination she knew he had within him. She met Ross's gaze, teeth worrying her lower lip. "I guess I've been afraid all these years that the same thing would happen to Teddy. He is passionate about the subject."

"All Little Leaguers are." Ross smiled in understanding. Again their hands touched, withdrew. "So what are you going to do?" Ross asked.

"Let him play." She folded and unfolded the napkin in her lap. "It's what Teddy needs, and that's what's important to me now. To tell you the truth, I didn't realize how much playing in the league meant to him until yesterday, when I asked him if he still wanted to go to that superdeluxe camp he's bugged me about for the past several years." Her son had been unable to confide in her on perhaps the very subject that mattered most to him, the father he never knew. "I realize now I will eventually have to tell him the truth about Ted." She took a deep breath. "In the long run it will be the kindest action to take. But I'll do it in bits and pieces, just give him as much as he wants to know and understand. I want him to hear it from me, Ross, when the time is right. So yes, he can still play on your team, providing he isn't harassed by the other boys."

Ross faced her determinedly. "I'll make sure of it. Though to be honest, after thinking about it, I don't think you have anything to worry about. Not until

Teddy is much older." Old enough to pursue his father's past life with real zeal.

"Thank you for being so understanding about all of this," she said quietly.

He shrugged off his concern for Teddy as nothing. "I see now why you were so upset about Teddy becoming involved in baseball. As for it becoming an obsessive interest, maybe you just need to balance out his interest in sports with other things. Like scouting or music lessons...."

"Don't tell me," she laughed. "You head up a scout troop too!"

"No, but I've been thinking about it."

"You're probably right about that. I'll look into it first chance I get, and see what extracurricular activities are available for someone his age." It surprised her to realize she felt steadier, more able to handle the complex demands of parenthood, just knowing Ross was around.

As the meal concluded, Ross said, "I'd like to be his Big Brother. Teddy needs a role model, someone to talk to and be with him man to man. I can do that for him."

There was a new ease between them, the comforting knowledge of having weathered a crisis together and coming out not only whole, but stronger for it. It seemed right for her to be there with him. Still, his suggestion caught her by surprise. "We can do it on an informal basis," he assured.

"Have you ever done this before, worked with another child?"

He shook his head. "Not specifically, not other than the work I've done coaching my softball team." His pragmatic tone seemed to imply he would take Teddy on as a companion with or without her as a romantic sidekick.

"Then why now?" she asked. Her heart seemed to be beating a hundred miles a minute.

Ross leaned back to allow a passing busboy to remove his plate. "Because I like Teddy. He reminds me of myself at that age. And I miss my own son, who's long since outgrown the stage of needing a father the way someone Teddy's age does." He leaned toward her persuasively. "I know how lonely it can be growing up without a father, Eileen. Teddy's a wonderful boy, exuberant and energetic. He deserves more than you're able to give as a mother."

There was no disputing Ross's logic. She knew her son already adored him. Stronger than the instinctive need to trust Ross was the fiercely maternal desire to protect Teddy from hurt. "It's a very generous offer, Ross, one I appreciate very much. But if he were to start relying on you too much—" Her voice caught. Teddy could easily make demands on Ross that the successful attorney might not have time to fill, souring the relationship for them both. As much as she wanted to see it happen, the cool logical side of her insisted she sound out Ross's feelings.

"Like you relied on your husband?" The insight was soft, yet cutting.

Swallowing hard, Eileen stirred additional lemon into her tea, avoiding his probing gaze. "Yes."

"I'd never hurt your son, Eileen. I'd never let him down."

She knew that. But still she was afraid. "Let me think about it," she said finally. Maybe Ross was right.

"Take all the time you need," he assured.

"Well, as long as Teddy's going to play softball, I'd like to be active in the league—maybe work in the concession stand or make phone calls, something like that," she suggested hesitantly.

Ross smiled his approval. "That's wonderful. The league can use all the help offered." He gave her the phone number of a woman to call. "By the way, there's a family and player picnic scheduled for Friday evening at the park. All the teams will be there. Teddy should probably attend." He looked down at her. "Would you like us all to go together? I can introduce you around."

"Thank you. I'd like that very much." She wondered if she'd be able to wait that long to see him again.

The drive back to work was accomplished all too swiftly. Ross halted the car in the back lot of the bank, then reached over to snap off the radio. The abrupt action left the car strangely quiet. She was aware of every rustle of breath, every slight sound. Again, her pulse throbbed.

"Thank you for the lunch, I enjoyed it," she said, feeling all at once strangely replete, as if just being with him had satisfied some deep, lonely void within her.

Looking as if he, too, were reluctant to let her go, he lifted a fingertip to the eighteen-carat-gold earring adorning her left lobe. "That's a very beautiful design," he murmured, tracing the leafy shape. He leaned closer, his gaze caressing her exposed earlobe. "Are those diamonds inset in the gold?"

"Yes." She blushed, ducking her head. After a moment, his hand dropped, but his steady gaze continued, focusing on the newly glossed shimmer of her mouth. She had the strong sensation he wanted to kiss her, but, wary of her co-workers filtering back into the rear entrance of the building, did not. After a moment, his attention returned to the jewelry adorning her ear.

"It's beautiful," he repeated. "I've never seen anything like it."

On impulse and because he was still staring with such fascination at her ear, Eileen swiftly undid the clasp. She held one pierced earring in her hand for better viewing. "I had them crafted according to a design I saw in *Vogue*. A friend of mine was an artist. She specialized in this kind of work." The exquisite jewelry was also her sole indulgence in a world geared mostly around her child.

Ross's index finger traced the maple leaf design, inadvertently brushing her palm in the process. "Does she still live here in town?" he asked, his voice a soft throaty caress.

"No," Eileen answered, refastening the diamond-adorned leaf on the lobe of her ear. The catch stuck for a moment, but with a little twisting slid obediently into place. "She moved away several years ago. The last I heard she was living out west, in one of the ski resorts in Colorado."

"Do you have any other designs she created?" he asked as she routinely gathered up her purse. "Anything else that caught your fancy?"

"No, this was my only pair of one-of-a-kind earrings," she confessed softly, her hand clutching the door latch as if it were a lifeline to safety. She cleared her throat. "I've really got to go."

"I'll call you later this evening, after Teddy's in bed," he promised. Leaning across her, he opened her door. "We'll talk about everything...anything. Whatever you want." They both knew the subject was irrelevant. He wanted to get to know her, and she desperately wanted to know more about him.

The temptation of a full-fledged affair loomed desperately close. "I'd like that," she said breathlessly. Before she could stop herself, she said, "Two dates in one meeting?"

Ross grinned. "I like to book ahead," he teased. A horn beeped from the car behind them. So engrossed were they in each other, they barely noticed the irate driver pull around them, frowning.

His fingers curled loosely around her wrist, sensually branding her skin with his unutterably tender touch. "I also want to spend some more time with Teddy, apart from the rest of the team, teach him the fundamentals of batting and help him get caught up with the other players his age. Are both of you free tomorrow night?"

"Yes." Heaven help her, she was falling in love again...and this time it was oh, so sweet...she didn't think she could bear it.

"Good. I'll pick you up at your place at five-thirty. We'll have a quick dinner first at McDonald's or someplace that Teddy would like." His thumb brushed with feather-light intensity over her wrist. Shivers started inside her and traveled with incredible power up and down her spine.

"He'd like that, I know." Unconsciously, she leaned into him, wanting his embrace.

His lips brushed hers, leaving a wealth of sensation behind. "So I'll see you again tomorrow night...and talk to you again later?"

"Yes." Oh, yes! Without warning, her life seemed a rainbow of possibilities. And no matter how busy the afternoon at work proved, the hours would never fly by swiftly enough to suit her. Eileen opened the door, got out of the car, and with a reluctant, final glance at him, strode off toward the bank.

It was nearly four in the afternoon before Eileen noticed with chagrin that her left earring, the one she had removed for a fraction of a second in Ross's car, was missing. She called Ross's office on the off chance that she might have dropped it in his car. His secretary told her he was in court, but promised to give him the message upon his return. Just to be safe, Eileen double-checked her path into the bank, the conference rooms and her private office. Nowhere did she find the valuable earring.

To her disappointment, Ross didn't return her call directly. "You sure are fidgety tonight, mom," Teddy observed later, after his bath. He was curled up in front of the television, sunburned, content, sleepily warding off bedtime. Teddy hid a yawn behind his hand.

Eileen smiled, taking the hint and sitting down on the sofa with the best-seller she was still trying to fin- ish. "Sorry, sport." She apologized for her dreamy agitation. "I just have a lot on my mind."

"Hmm," Teddy said. Minutes later, he was almost sound asleep. Eileen coaxed him up off his self- styled bed of throw pillows and ushered him up- stairs to his room.

Ross dropped by unannounced around ten-thirty, and Eileen's mood automatically lifted at the sight of him. He looked weary, as if he'd spent most of the evening at the office. An evening's growth of beard outlined his jaw. Eileen felt immediately guilty for having made him go so far out of his way over what must have seemed a very trivial errand. Or worse yet, possibly even an unsubtle feminine ploy for his attention.

"Rough day?" she murmured sympathetically. To her astonishment, she sounded like a woman wel- coming her man home.

He nodded and leaned down until his mouth met hers in a brief soft kiss. She tasted mint and the salty tang of his skin. "The worst." He drew back slightly to assess her visually. His thumbs swept across her cheekbones, his fingertips rested beneath her chin and tilted her face back beneath his. "Better now that I'm here." He kissed her again then, ever so reluctantly, released her.

"The reason I called you earlier—" she began.

He braced one shoulder against the frame, both hands held palm up in a gesture of surrender. "No luck finding it so far," he reported matter-of-factly. "Are you sure you lost the earring in my car?"

She shook her head. "No. I'm not. But the last place I can remember having them both on is in your car."

Ross sighed his frustration, threading his fingers through his hair. "I know why you'd hate to lose them. Aside from the artistry involved, they looked very valuable."

Taking his arm, she ushered him inside, admitting on a sigh, "It's more than just the money or the fact that a friend of mine made them. It's the sentimental value attached to them, too. They've been kind of a good-luck charm to me. I got them about five years ago, when Teddy was four. After having been on my own for nearly four and a half years, the struggle of being a single parent and career woman was really wearing me down. Plus, I was taking some business courses at the university three nights a week so I could work my way up from teller to loan officer. I decided to purchase the earrings on a layaway plan, and then for every week I made it through I paid another small amount. By the time I had finished paying for them I'd also earned my associate business degree. After that, it seemed to get easier. I earned my bachelor's last year."

He smiled in understanding. "Did you buy your-

self a diamond necklace to match, in way of con-
gratulations?''

''No.''

He paused, catching her wrist in his palm, then
suggested humorously, ''They say the third time's
the charm. Maybe we'll get lucky if we look for the
earring together.'' They strolled out to the car together, not quite touching, yet miraculously in sync
considering the difference in their heights. It pleased
her to have him measure his strides to hers so effortlessly.

Eileen held the flashlight while he bent and rummaged around in the car. Unfortunately, no matter
how much they scrambled around they couldn't lo-
cate the missing gold-leaf earring. ''I'm afraid it's
lost for good,'' Eileen said with a grimace. ''The back
on the clasp has been loose for some time. I've just
delayed getting it fixed.''

Ross's mouth tightened. ''I feel responsible.'' He
sighed. ''If I hadn't asked you about them, you never
would have taken that one off.''

She waved off his concern as they strode slowly
back toward the house. ''Don't be silly. For all I know
I could have lost them sitting at my desk at the bank
this afternoon. In fact, I probably did.'' She shrugged.
''Maybe it'll turn up overnight. Maybe the cleaning
people will find it. I left them a note.''

''Maybe,'' he agreed, sounding unconvinced.

The porch light shone like a halo above their
heads, illuminating them for all the neighborhood to
see. Drawing her over into the shadows, Ross bent
his head to hers. ''I know it's just been hours since I
saw you,'' he murmured, ''but to me it seems like
days. I'm glad you called.'' Their lips touched, and
she clung to him, returning the sensual caress for

long moments. Tremors shook her body along with the deep need for greater intimacy, and she knew that she wanted to make love to him here and now with all her heart and soul. Yet to begin an affair with Ross would bring too many complications to a life that seemed sometimes to be vastly overburdened. She needed to think it through when she wasn't under his sensual spell. "Ross, I—" Hands clasping his forearms, she broke the embrace.

"I understand the timing's all wrong." His gaze traversed her slowly. "When?" The word was taut with frustration.

For that, she had no answer and would make no promises. "I don't know."

Gently, he touched an index finger to her lips. "Think about me tonight, Eileen. Think about us and what could be. That's all I ask. And will ask, until you're ready to commit yourself to more." He hugged her to him once more, his arms solid and secure around her, his mouth tenderly brushing her temple. And then, before she could protest, he was gone.

5

"KEEP YOUR WRISTS LOOSE NOW," Ross coached Teddy gently, reaching around him and grasping the boy's forearms to demonstrate what he meant. "Atta boy. You can't hit what you can't see so keep your head up...not too close to the base now...that's it... that's it...."

Eileen smiled. Ross's suggestion of turning catch-up batting practice into a miniouting for all three was working out terrifically. Dinner had been a delightful repast of hamburgers, French fries and chocolate shakes eaten in the shady confines of the city park. After a suitable interval, they'd gotten the mitts and bats out of his car. As Eileen watched, Ross was patiently instructing an exuberant Teddy on the fundamentals of hitting. It warmed her heart to see Teddy so happy, basking in the glow of Ross's attention. She saw now how much had been missing in Teddy's life. Ross could fill that void.

Her attention returned to home plate. Hair shoved back from his forehead, Teddy had his baseball cap pulled down low over his brow. Ross was showing him how to swing. "Follow through on it...that's it...that's it...." Releasing his grip on her son, Ross looked up abruptly. "Either I need to be two places at once or we need some help, sport—someone to catch." Grinning, he shot Eileen an inspired glance.

Slinking down in her seat, Eileen shot back, "I was afraid you'd suggest that." Nonetheless she stood obediently and, dusting the grass off the seat of her pants, started their way. "I warn you, I have no athletic talents whatsoever."

"She's right, Mr. Mitchell," Teddy agreed ruefully.

"That's all right, Teddy, anyone can learn." And Ross so wanted to be her teacher.

Teddy smothered a giggle behind his hand. "You don't know mom. She can't even hit the wastebasket with a spitball—from a distance of three feet."

Ross shook his head at her in mock dismay. "Why, you poor, deprived woman."

"Disheartening, isn't it?" She grinned. "Do you want me to catch?"

"Actually, I'd rather you pitched," Ross decided. "That way I can stand behind Teddy and help him improve his swing, as well as chase stray balls."

"Knowing mom, there are going to be a lot of stray balls." Teddy giggled again. In response, Ross pulled the bill of Teddy's hat down over his brow.

"Give your mom half a chance," Ross scolded playfully when Teddy had pushed the hat back off his face and could see again. He turned toward Eileen. "You can pitch, can't you? Sure you can," he decided, not giving her a chance to admit that Teddy's opinion just might be the more accurate assessment of her abilities. Sensing her unease, Ross pulled off his Running Tigers cap and placed it over her head, then thumped a softball mitt in one hand and ball in the other. Turning her around toward the pitcher's mound, he pointed her in the general direction and gave her a nudge.

"I'm no great shakes as a pitcher," she warned Ross.

"About time you learned, then, don't you think?" Ross pronounced firmly.

"Yeah, mom, 'bout time you learned," Teddy

echoed, gazing fixedly out at the pitcher's mound. His expression was serious. She knew he was thinking about his hitting.

Pete and Re-peat, she thought wryly. And although Teddy was good, she knew with practice he could be better. "Okay." She pounded the ball into her glove with a flourish. "Where do I throw it?" She fixed Ross and Teddy with a teasingly innocent look.

Both males groaned. "Toward the batter."

"At him?" Eileen asked, lightly paying Teddy back for his earlier wit. Teddy moaned and stared skyward.

"That would be a foul play," Ross pronounced dryly, watching her adjust his hat sideways across her head. "In more ways than one."

Now it was Eileen's turn to groan. "Do bad puns count or only bad plays?"

"Very funny, lady. Just pitch." He fixed her with a mock scowl.

Teddy, witnessing the exchange, was giggling again. Shaking his head, he said finally, "Come on, mom, just pitch!" He impatiently swung the bat.

"Okay." Eileen took a deep breath. "Here goes." Her first ball landed about three feet to the side of home plate. Teddy rolled his eyes skyward and made a great show of stomping his feet. Ross blinked in disbelief, then chased after the ball. Eileen cleared her throat. "Maybe I'd better get a little closer," she said.

"Maybe you'd better," Ross agreed dryly.

The second pitch sailed over home plate, about a foot too high. Teddy didn't even bother to swing. Watching it bounce as the ball hit first the backstop and then the ground, Teddy shook his head in mock disbelief. "And I thought I needed extra practice. Gosh, mom!"

Eileen flushed, embarrassed. "A little lower," Ross said, strolling toward her. "Relax." He tossed her the ball. She caught it in her mitt. His eyes met hers and she saw, suddenly, the same tender tutelage he had bestowed on her son. "Try pitching underhand," he advised softly. "It's easier to control the ball."

Suddenly, she felt capable of mastering anything. "All right." Under Ross's patient instruction she managed to do a fair job of pitching. Teddy hit roughly half of all she threw.

"Now remember," Ross said, giving Teddy an encouraging pat on the shoulder. "Always follow the ball. Keep your shoulders back, your wrists loose, a comfortable grip on the bat...you'll do fine." With sudden mischief, Ross sent Eileen a droll look. "Of course the pitcher for the opposing team is going to be a lot tougher to beat than your mom," he teased.

"And he'll be standing on the mound, too," Teddy said, half seriously.

Gloved hand on her hip, Eileen jovially faced the two men in her life. It was good to see Teddy enjoying himself so much. "Okay, coach, enough of this 'back seat' pitching. Let's see what you can do!" She assumed the catcher's position behind home plate.

With relish he accepted her challenge to show Teddy how tough the competition was really going to be. "Don't mind if I do," he said. Snatching back his Running Tigers hat, he pulled it low over his brow. To Teddy's delight and Eileen's comically feigned chagrin, he swaggered theatrically back to the mound and once there made a great show of warming up, squinting, flexing and generally clowning around. Eventually, when Teddy's laughter had quieted, Ross got down to business. Eileen was amazed at the controlled ease with which he threw and Teddy's attention as he gave his all during practice. Finally, around eight, they called a halt.

"Thanks for helping me tonight," Teddy said shyly as they gathered up the equipment.

Ross gazed down at him tenderly, then aimed a gentle punch at his shoulder. "Anytime, sport." He offered his palm. "Put her there." In lieu of handshakes, they exchanged youthfully macho slaps of the palm.

"I'll put the stuff in the car." Teddy's eyes were shining as he raced off.

"I haven't seen him looking this happy since I don't know when," Eileen said softly when Teddy was out of earshot. She touched the swell of muscle above Ross's elbow. "Thank you."

"It was my pleasure, believe me." His gaze lingered on her mouth. "We'll have to do it again sometime soon."

"I'd like that."

"Me too." Suddenly Eileen didn't want the evening to end.

"Would I be rushing you if I asked to see you again later this evening?" Ross asked, appearing to have read her mind. "After Teddy's in bed?" He looked down at his athletic clothes. "I'd like to go home and shower first."

And she needed to get Teddy settled for the night. But there was nothing she wanted more than to be with him. And it had to do with a lot more than simple gratitude for the time he had spent with Teddy. She wanted the intimacy they'd generated to continue, but she wanted it on a different, higher level. And she was afraid, as he seemed to be, that if they waited too long or delayed, the newfound closeness would fade. "Shall we say ten o'clock?" Ross asked softly as they joined Teddy at the car.

"Sounds good." Eileen smiled.

Teddy was exhausted. He bathed while Eileen showered and changed. "Is Ross coming over later?" he asked sleepily, climbing into bed without complaint.

"For a short while," Eileen admitted. Teddy didn't seem to mind. In fact, he welcomed the visit, although he was not to be included. That, too, was a first, she mused. He'd always resented her few escorts before. But none of them had taken the time with Teddy that Ross had, and none had his gift for communicating one-to-one.

"I'm glad. I like him." Teddy snuggled down into the covers, his arms folded behind his head. His hair was damp and smelled of baby shampoo. His blue eyes focused on her like twin laser beams. "You had a good time tonight, didn't you, mom? Even though all we were doing was playing baseball." He knew it was a sport she had previously hated.

"Yes, I did." She paused, knowing it was time to explain her previous resentment of the sport. "I know it seems I've been unreasonable about baseball in the past."

"How come?" He wanted only to understand, not to judge.

Eileen was struck with the depth of his compassion. She shrugged. "I don't know. I guess because the memories made me sad, reminded me of my loss. I wish your dad and I had been blessed with more time together." She wished they'd had the time to make it right between them again or, at the very least, make a clean break, one not so fraught with guilt and what-ifs or might-have-beens. She clasped Teddy's hand between both of hers, admitting with heartfelt honesty, "I wish he'd had the chance to know you. I think it would have made a big difference in his life."

Teddy nodded, sadly accepting. "I wish I'd known

dad, too." His chin lifted earnestly as he sought to make her understand his point of view. "That's why I wanted to play Little League so much, mom. Baseball makes me feel closer to dad."

Eileen smoothed the hair from his brow. "I know. And he would have been very proud of you." She realized with a start there had been a lot of love in the past after all. The bitterness had come only at the very end. Now it was time, finally, to truly accept what had happened and go forward, without looking back.

Teddy hesitated. "Was dad a failure because he was sent to the farm league, mom?"

Eileen shook her head, choosing her words carefully. "No, but it wasn't what he'd dreamed it would be, either. I think he regretted that he didn't finish college, pay more attention to his studies."

"So he could have done something else, then, like be a lawyer or a teacher," Teddy surmised solemnly.

"Eventually, yes, most athletes do. Which is why I want you to be prepared."

Teddy smothered a yawn behind his hand, as if sensing an impending maternal minilecture on the importance of responsibility. "I promise I won't let my grades slip, mom, or be lazy at school." His eyes gleamed in a way that was suddenly very much like Ross. "But you have to promise me something, too."

Eileen tucked the covers around him. She sensed a pun about to be thrown her way. "What?"

"That you'll learn more about baseball. The silly way you pitch...!" Giggling, he ducked her gentle chuck on the chin and, still laughing, suffered through a tousling of his hair.

"Okay, young man, sleep!" Eileen said, switching off his light.

"Good night, mom." Teddy's voice came sleepily

out of the dark. "And thanks for being such a good sport and coming along with us tonight."

"You're welcome."

SWIFTLY, EILEEN APPLIED blush, mascara and lip gloss. She ran a brush through her hair and then, satisfied with her appearance, applied her favorite perfume. Teddy was sleeping soundly by the time she was through. She gazed down at him in the dark, feeling so very lucky to have him.

Downstairs again, she put a bottle of wine on ice and hastily but expertly prepared a tray of hot cheese canapés. At exactly ten, there was a soft knock at the door. Her heart pounding in anticipation, Eileen moved to the door. Ross stood on the threshold, eyes caressing her slender form as if he'd never be able to look at her long enough to suit him. Freshly showered and shaven, he was dressed casually, in snug-fitting white tennis shorts, and a navy-blue golf shirt. As always, he looked incredibly attractive. His stance was virile and completely at ease.

"Hello."

"Hi." Her greeting was cut off by the swift, sure descent of his lips. When she could breathe again, he moved past her and closed the door. Eileen's breath caught in her chest. She knew she was taking a step from which there would be no return—but she didn't care. She wanted to be with him, near him again. Nothing else seemed important. His eyes lovingly checked out the gauzy apricot bandeau top and roved down over the flatness of her abdomen beneath the white cotton drawstring shorts. Her toes were bare, making her feel even more vulnerable and open to his sensual inspection. His gaze drifted over the curling disarray of her golden-brown hair.

It was the first time he'd seen her with her hair up. Involuntarily, Eileen lifted a hand to the careless knot on top of her head, self-consciously brushing at the tendrils curving across her cheek and down the back of her neck. He tracked the movement like a starving man. "You look incredibly lovely," he murmured huskily. His voice was the softest caress.

"Thank you. You look... wonderful, too." Though their conversation was hopelessly inane, it seemed perfectly appropriate. "I thought we'd sit out on the patio. It's such a lovely night."

"Teddy's asleep?" His hand touched her spine as they strolled into her kitchen.

"Yes. He was exhausted," Eileen murmured, knowing that Ross wasn't—and neither was she.

Ross helped her carry the tray containing their drinks. Eileen removed her canapés from the oven and, after arranging them nicely on a platter, followed him out the door. Gallantly, he shut the sliding glass door on a resolute whoosh. As the drapes to the kitchen were still closed, the patio was shrouded in semidarkness. Eileen bent to light a scented candle on the patio table. The air was muggy and soft, caressing her skin like a warm balm. They sat at the white, lacy cast-iron table. Eileen realized she felt more at peace with herself than she had in a long time, and she had Ross to thank. Wanting him to know what had transpired between her and her son, she said softly, "I had a talk with Teddy tonight about Ted." Ross lifted his head alertly.

Pouring them each some wine, she continued in a subdued tone, "We talked about my prejudice against baseball." She grinned. "My son thinks I just might be getting over it."

"I think so, too," Ross agreed happily.

Eileen smiled. "I realized most of my bitterness

stemmed from the fact that I never had a chance to make our marriage work or correct the flaws." She held up a hand to prevent his consoling interruption. "I'm not saying Ted and I could have made a go of it over the long haul.... In retrospect, probably not. But at least I would've known that I did everything possible. If Teddy's father had known his son, he might have felt different about his future...it might have offered an incentive to go on and build a solid future for himself. Then I wouldn't have felt so responsible...." She trailed off, her voice thick with unshed tears.

He reached across the table to cover her free hand with his own. As he spoke, he softly stroked her skin. "I know what you mean, both from personal experience and dealing in my law practice." Her eyes lifted, warming with understanding. He continued gently, "As surviving spouses, whether from death or divorce, the going is always hard later, fraught with guilt and feelings of failure. Knowing as I eventually did that my ex-wife had gone on to make a nice, stable life for herself—one she never would have had with me had we stayed together—lessened my anxiety. Because what she wanted, I never could have given her, or even helped her get. Fortunately for both of us, she was smart enough to realize that and get out of the relationship even while I protested." His mouth twisted ruefully. "Of course, if she'd messed up hopelessly on her own, I probably would have jumped in to save her, just out of guilt or duty. But part of growing up is learning that you can't take responsibility for another adult's actions, Eileen...ultimately we're all on our own. In other words, stop blaming yourself for something only your husband had the power to change. Guilt would have been counterproductive then. It's detrimental to both you and Teddy now."

She nodded slowly, absorbing the wisdom of all he had said. "I'm fortunate to have heard your story." It was good to know his situation had worked out all right—for both of them. "I guess there's no predicting fate, is there?"

He rose, catching her arm and pulling her up and around to face him. His arms wound around her like bands of flame. "Not unless it's what I want of you right now, have been wanting for what seems like a lifetime...."

His head bent to just a fraction above hers, and his free arm circled her waist, lightly massaging her back. Eileen felt her bare legs brush the hair-roughened surface of his. Her breasts were crushed against the solid contours of his chest. "Love me, Eileen," Ross implored softly. She sensed his request was for more than just physical satisfaction—and she gladly complied. His hands came up to frame her face. He cupped a hand around her nape, his thumb lightly brushing the skin beneath her ear. His touch at first was teasing and light then swiftly became deeper and more commanding. His mouth lowered to hers, and once he kissed her, the right of refusal was lost, buried in the smoldering passion they found. By halting steps he glided her backward to the chaise, so that she was lying beneath him, her open thighs making a cradle for his sinewy length. Everywhere they touched, an electric current vibrated. Ross's hands lovingly trespassed beneath the filmy top she wore and caressed her bare midriff and gentle curves, her taut peaking nipples. As slowly as if they had all the time in the world instead of only fleeting minutes, he explored the satiny expanse of skin between her shoulder blades. His palms traveled lower, past her waist, then across her hips, cupping her to him. His weight covered hers, his legs sliding in to nestle more closely between her open thighs. He shifted until there was no doubting his need of her or the perfect fit of their bodies. His mouth devoured hers then teased and caressed, evoking a wealth of sensations.

"You feel so good," he asserted, feeling her trembling response. His eyes skimmed all of her. Raising a hand to her hair, he loosened the coil of soft brown hair. Removing the pins one by one, he threaded his fingers through the luxuriant length, not stopping until the shimmering mass feathered her face in a halo of his design.

"So do you." Eileen felt as if she'd been weighted down irrevocably. She lay absolutely still, her eyes closing, as if that would lock out the feel of his body. He remained prone over her, a disturbingly exciting sensation. Eileen felt utterly incapable of resisting him as his hands slid up over her rib cage. Tremors ran through her body, underscoring the need to let go, give in. She wanted to be swept away, to travel to the ardent heights only he could take her.

The scent of newly bloomed roses hung heavy in the air, adding to her sweet lethargy. His thumbs teased the crests of her nipples and she arched against him, feeling every hot, hard plane. "Oh, Ross," she moaned. His mouth lifted ever so slightly at the corners. Even in the dim light, she could see the gleam of male triumph in his eyes, followed by the more complex emotions of tenderness mingling with his desire.

"Don't stop me now," he murmured, echoing aloud her need, "not when I want you this badly." His mouth shifted again, trailing fire down her neck, kissing her, seducing, and when she could barely breathe, drifted lower still. He kissed her breasts through the cloth, wetting the fabric, transporting her into a world of sensual pleasure, making her gasp and cry out and cradle his head next to her throbbing bosom.

"Make love with me, Eileen." Again, his hands moved under her shirt to claim her, his palms flattening beneath her spine, pressing her closer still. The time to make the decision had come, Eileen knew. She either continued to full intimacy or called a halt entirely.

The sound of slamming car doors and voices from the neighboring street intruded. He paused, lifting his head, and looked at her. She could invite him in, she knew. Or she could stay there and make love with him on the patio. No one would know. In the darkness, no one would be able to see. Even if they did, she wasn't sure she would have cared, if it hadn't been for Teddy. Suppose he woke. Suppose. "Ross, no, not with Teddy just upstairs."

"You're right, of course." His withdrawal, both physical and emotional, was abrupt. "Teddy shouldn't ever see you in a compromising position. I'm sorry if it seemed I was trying to seduce you into irresponsibility where your son was concerned."

Tears of frustration filled her eyes. She hated to leave it like this between them, both of them aching and unfulfilled. She turned her head away and swallowed hard, not knowing what to say. "It's all right," he soothed, covering her hand. The soft intensity of his words let her know it truly was all right. "I'd rather wait until the moment is exactly right before making love with you. I want it to be everything you and I both ever dreamed possible, not a hurried tryst, with both of us worrying about discovery." Ross moved to sit beside her, waiting as she readjusted her clothing.

His hand gently brushed at an errant strand of her hair. She had an odd wish to press his hand against her face, just hold it to her, savoring his warmth. She didn't, only because she didn't trust herself not to kiss him again, and then again. And if they started, she knew there would be no stopping.

"Thank you...for being such a gentleman," she said awkwardly at last, ducking her head shyly.

"I care about you, Eileen, very much."

"And I care about you."

The truth was she loved him. But it was too soon for her to say the words aloud, even to herself. And she didn't want to scare him away. Graciously she walked him to the door. He moved closer. His palms stroked languorously up her spine, sending up a blast of heat wherever he touched.

"We've still got a date for the picnic Friday evening, don't forget," he whispered in her ear.

She turned her face up to his for another long kiss. "I won't." And even if she were able to forget, which was unlikely, Teddy would remind her constantly. "Will I see you before then?" she asked huskily. She wanted, irrationally, to spend every waking hour at his side. She yearned to get to know him more intimately than any man.

At her question, Ross grimaced. He held her away from him slightly, watching her reaction. "My next few days are going to be very hectic," he admitted. "That's one of the reasons I've crammed so much activity into the past two days." At the unsettled expression on her face, he explained, "One of the junior attorneys in my firm is having her first court case early next week. She's got a lot of potential, but her court presence needs polishing. I'll be working with her to build her confidence and prepare the case. I have to go over the briefs and affidavits she's prepared and also work with her on the opening and closing statements to the jury, such as they are at the moment.''

Eileen felt an uncomfortable twinge of jealousy. It faded abruptly as Ross took her back into his arms, his hand soothingly stroking the back of her neck. His lips brushed her temple, her cheek. "If I do this, I'll have the whole weekend to spend with you and Teddy. Can you understand?'' He held her at arm's length. Clearly it was important to him that she comprehend his devotion to his work.

Because she felt the same about her career, she relaxed. "Of course. Which isn't to say I won't miss being with you—''

"I'll call you late every night, after you're in bed.''

She leaned into him for one last joyous embrace. "I'd like that, very much.''

6

"MOM, WILL YOU HURRY UP? We're going to be late!"
Teddy shouted from the top of the stairs.

Eileen raced down the steps, clutching her espa-
drilles in her hand. "I'm hurrying, I'm hurrying!"
Of all nights to have a crisis at the bank, she thought.
Teddy had been frantic by the time she arrived at
Janey's to pick him up. He was worried that he'd
miss his big evening with Ross and the team.

"Give your mother a chance to catch her breath,"
Ross observed from just outside the screen door. Eileen glanced at him gratefully. For an instant their
eyes met, and she felt the searing sensation all the
way to her bare painted toes.

"Thanks for the backup." She smiled, happy to see
him. Though they had talked every night on the
phone, this was the first time she had seen him in
three days. She felt so happy it was incredible. Peace
stole over her, the effect of just having Ross nearby.

"Bad day at the office?" he asked as she ushered
him in. His steps, usually fast and determined, were
deliberately slow.

"The worst." She grimaced. She knew he yearned
to kiss her, and she yearned to embrace him, too.
Aware of Teddy's round saucer eyes, however, she
was suddenly shy. A corner of Ross's mouth lifted in
a wry smile, and she knew he understood—more,
respected the care with which she treated Teddy's
feelings. It would be hard for Teddy to learn to share

his mother with another man unless they took it slow and easy and took pains to include him, too.

Placing her hand on the swell of muscle above his elbow, she bent to slip on first one shoe, then the other. Still feeling breathless and flushed, she straightened. "The credit bureau lost another whole series of reports which, if they hadn't been found, would have delayed roughly twenty loan applications. I had to go all the way up the chain of command at my office and down through their ranks to get it straightened out."

He smiled down at her, his expression telling her he had already accurately guessed the outcome of the business squabble. "And did you?"

She nodded triumphantly, glad to be able to share her professional success with another adult. "You bet. I may have had to work late, but the employees at fault at the credit bureau are going to have to work later." They both broke into laughter.

"Hi, Teddy, how are you doing?" Ross paused to greet her son specifically.

Teddy beamed. "Fine." He turned back to Eileen, though much mollified simply by Ross's presence and attention, still slightly aggrieved. "Mom, your wristwatch is on upside down."

"Oh!" Flushing, she twisted the flexible band back off and put it on right side up. "Anything else on backward or upside down?" She'd showered briskly and changed clothes so hurriedly there was no predicting.

"You look fine to me," Ross observed with a twinkle in his eye. He turned to Teddy. "What do you think, sport?"

"She looks fine to me, too. More than fine! Let's go!" He grabbed both their wrists and started towing them both toward the door.

"Whoa, partner," Ross said, reeling Teddy back in to his side. Placing both hands on the boy's shoulders, he radiated calm. "We've got time yet."

"I don't want to be late," Teddy pouted hesitantly.

"We won't be," Ross assured.

"Well...." Teddy frowned again, but Eileen could tell the battle was already won.

"I promised him I'd be home early," she explained, going into the kitchen to gather up the food and utensils she had pledged to bring. Both males followed.

"She didn't have time to make potato salad," Teddy reported.

For that, she was sorry. Yet she realized how impractical it would have been. After all, she only had two hands and multiple demands on her time. Eileen faced Ross. She didn't want either male to think she didn't know how important an event this was, or that she was being deliberately difficult, as she had been in the past about anything even faintly connected with baseball. "I stopped at the delicatessen on my way home. Do you think that will be all right?"

"I'm sure it will be." Ross paused, sensing she needed a few more minutes to recoup after her long day. "If you like, Teddy and I can run an errand. That will give you another half hour or so. And," he added before Teddy could mournfully interrupt, "I promise you we still won't be late. I know for a fact we won't eat until much later. So, what do you say, sport? Are you game for a short run?"

"Sure." Teddy linked hands with Ross, then relaxed into his embrace as Ross's arm circled his shoulder again. Eileen smiled at the affection between them.

"Thank you." Eileen sighed. "I'll be ready to go when you get back, I promise."

"Don't worry about it." Ross smiled. "I know how to keep this young man amused. I know this videogame place—"

"Really, Ross?" Teddy exclaimed as they headed out the front door.

They were gone roughly forty-five minutes. When they came back in the door, Teddy was carrying a large paper bag and grinning from ear to ear. She knew they were up to something. And it had to do with more than whatever electronic game Ross had let Teddy play—and probably let win.

"Guess what we got, mom?" Teddy prompted, his eyes shining.

"I don't know. Not...more potato salad?"

"No." Teddy glanced up at Ross for confirmation, then getting the nod that the timing was right, thrust the bag into her lap.

"Open it," Ross said softly, strolling over casually to stand beside the sofa. Teddy plopped down on the other side of her. "It's from both of us," Ross finished softly.

Slowly, she uncovered a brand-new baseball cap and a golden leather glove. "We figured if you were going to join the home team and learn how to play and pitch and bat right, you needed your own glove and hat," Teddy reported gleefully. "One that says Running Tigers, too."

"So you won't have to keep borrowing mine," Ross added.

"And we're going to practice a lot from now on," Teddy reported.

"All three of us," Ross said.

Tears welled up unexpectedly in the corners of her eyes. "I don't know what to say," she murmured huskily at last. The sense of family they'd created was everything she could have wished for.

"Thanks will do nicely," Teddy prompted, paro-
dying one of her favorite expressions with a pleased
grin.

"Thank you both." She stood and reached out to
give them both a kiss and a hug.

"Now we'd really better go," Ross said, gathering
the foil-wrapped container she had placed on the
counter next to her purse. "Or contrary to my word,
we will be late!"

Teddy's excitement mounted as they made the
short drive to the ball park. He walked obediently, if
a bit impatiently, with them through the crammed
parking lot to the edge of the grass, then cast his
mother a pleading glance. "Go play with your
friends." She gave her permission readily. "But be
careful! And watch where you're going!" With the
proliferation of bats, gloves and balls around it was
definitely a danger zone, albeit a youthful one.

"I will!" He raced off with an Indian war whoop.

"So much for motherly influence," she said dryly.
"Thank you for taking him off my hands earlier,"
Eileen said.

Ross laced his hand around hers and gave it an
affectionate squeeze. "My pleasure. Teddy really is a
delightful child."

"But he can be a handful."

"Aren't they all?"

The dusky glow of approaching sunset bathed
the nearby woods and playground equipment. Hot
dogs roasted in the charcoal-scented air. In the distance, some of the parents and sons had organized
an impromptu softball game. Together they strolled
toward the picnic benches under the covered shelter.

Hugh Deveraux was standing over a barbecue
grill, engaged in a conversation with his wife and

several other coaches and spouses. Chef's apron on, he was cooking the first of the hot dogs that would be served to the boys. Spying them, Janey waved and motioned them over. While Ross talked to Hugh, Eileen took both their culinary contributions to the buffet, which was currently being organized. Janey tagged along.

"The three of you looked very cozy when you arrived," she observed with her tell-big-sister-all look. "So, how is it going between you and Ross? Splendidly, I gather."

Self-consciously Eileen removed an icy, covered salad and insulated container of baked beans, aware that Ross was watching her. "Is it that obvious?" She knew she felt like she was walking on air whenever she was with Ross, that she had a perpetual grin on her face, which seemed at times impossible to suppress.

"More than," Janey announced. Together, they went to work, sorting out the casseroles on the green wooden tables. Eileen spread out the table linens and Janey organized the dishes according to category: entrée, side dish, hot, cold, salads, condiments and desserts. The other women iced the soft drinks and lined up plastic utensils, paper plates, napkins and Styrofoam cups.

Finished, the two sisters strolled over to a far corner of the shelter and took a seat in the shade, grateful for the chance to converse alone and without interruption. "So why were you late?" Janey wanted to know.

"You're beginning to sound like Teddy," Eileen teased. "Work complications, what else?" She went on to explain her latest victory against the incompetent management at the credit bureau. Janey nodded attentively, but she had a concerned look in her eyes.

"How did Ross react?" Janey asked cautiously.
"He didn't mind?"

"No, why should he?" Eileen faced Janey. "You
know something I don't—I can tell. Confess!"

"That's the reason he and his wife broke up—she
wanted to spend more time building her own career." Eileen paled. Janey rushed on consolingly,
"Don't panic. I didn't mean to upset you. It's just
that for a while afterward, Ross was very touchy on
the subject, slightly antagonistic to all women who
worked...obsessively. It was kind of a knee-jerk
reaction with him. Later, of course, when he'd re-
covered from his hurt, he did a complete turn-
around. I know he's since done more for equal rights
and equal pay than any other lawyer in the state.
He's got a reputation for defending women in both
civil and personal suits. I thought you were aware of
that."

"I knew about his legal reputation, yes. What
woman in this city doesn't? But as for his personal
life, I had no idea he felt that way...." Her voice
trailed off lamely. Had she misread him after all?
Was that the reason he'd rushed Teddy out of the
house and made up that errand? No, the gift had
been genuine, from the heart. He had to have
changed his opinion about women who worked.

"Look, for the record, I'm not surprised Ross
didn't confide in you." Janey hesitated, her faith in
Ross obviously complete. Eileen relaxed. Janey was a
fine judge of character. If she respected Ross so
much, he had more than earned her high opinion.
"He tends to keep his problems as well as his ac-
complishments under wraps. The first for reasons of
privacy, the second because he's a genuinely modest
person." She stood and stretched lazily. "You did
know Ross was being honored tomorrow evening at

the civic club, didn't you? He's been named Man of the Year, for outstanding leadership and community service."

Again, Eileen shook her head mutely. "We've talked every night this week."

Janey shook her head in despair, regretting she'd opened her big mouth. "And you didn't know that, either." She laughed. "Well, you've got to admit it isn't the easiest subject to work into the conversation." Adopting the voice of a conceited buffoon, she mimicked, "'Oh, by the way, *I'm* being honored for....'" The tension broken, they burst into giggles. Eileen had to admit that was definitely not Ross's style.

"Seriously, though," Janey continued, "I'm so glad to see you and Ross together. He was very hurt when his marriage broke up. He went through a rough time and ran through a lot of women, none of them exactly the type you would take home to meet mom and pop. It's nice to see him with a romantic gleam in his eye. Hugh's noticed the difference, too. Do you know he fairly glows every time he looks at you?"

Eileen flushed, warmth flooding her face. "You're joking."

As was her nature, Janey didn't pull any punches. "No, I'm not. And you're thinking matrimony, too, I can tell."

Ross and Hugh strolled over to join them. "What's the powwow about?" Ross asked, placing his hands caressingly on Eileen's shoulders. She became even warmer, though it was altogether a different, more primitive kind of heat flooding her limbs.

Janey laughed and stretched lazily. "I'm extolling your virtues, Mr. Mitchell!"

Ross drew back, hands raised traffic-officer style.

"Don't let me interrupt! Please, by all means, continue!" Everyone laughed.

Janey shook her head and pointed toward Eileen. "Where this woman is concerned, you don't need any help, counselor. She thinks you're Superman as it is."

"Is that true?" Ross asked when they were alone again.

Eileen knew she had nothing to lose by admitting it. "Yes."

Ross sat next to her, his jean-clad thigh nudging hers. He wore a navy-blue-and-white rugby shirt, its sleeves pushed past his elbows. The front placket was carelessly open, and dark hair curled from it, emphasizing the fit contours of his shoulders and chest. Suddenly, a need to touch him shot through Eileen, potent and compelling as a live electric wire. His eyes caressed her face, and she saw that he had missed her in the few minutes they'd been apart, as much as she had missed him.

"I have a confession to make," he said softly, eyes searching her face. "Hugh and I were talking about you, too. It's gotten to the point now where he accuses me of not being able to think about anything but you. And he's right—you're on my mind, constantly." His low voice warmed the insides of her thighs. "You haunt my dreams. You are my dreams."

A shiver started inside her, working its way through her limbs. She hugged her arms tightly beneath her breasts.

Ross's eyes wandered over her reminiscently, longingly. As his knee nudged hers, she was reminded of the differences between them, the hardness of his muscles when compared with her firm but softer legs. How would it feel to wrap her arms and legs around him, to wake up with their limbs cozily entwined?

His eyes swept over her lacy boat-necked aqua sweater and matching tailored linen pants. "You know, that light blue-green color highlights your hazel eyes in a most arresting way." A cool damp wind whipped across her as darkness fell. They could have been alone in the park for all the attention they paid to others. Her nipples were prominent against the delicately knit sweater and even thinner bra. He noticed. "Did you bring a jacket?" he asked, his voice solicitously low.

She shook her head mutely. "No."

"I've got a sweatshirt in my Jeep." He stood and started toward the parking lot, then without warning did an abrupt about-face, came back and hooked a hand around her waist. "On second thought," he said, casting a possessive glance at the other single men within the immediate vicinity, "maybe you'd better come with me." It thrilled her to know he felt that strongly about her, and together they strode swiftly to the Jeep, Ross leading the way. Once there, he swung her around by the waist and in the darkness of the parking lot, backed her up by achingly slow degrees against the side of the Jeep, adjusting her just so. His thighs straddled hers, holding her in hard masculine warmth. The pressure of his desire was insistent, and passion coursed through her.

Her hands moved up to create a wedge between them. "You're asking me to kiss you here? Now?" Her voice wavered breathlessly. Although they were alone, sheltered from view for the moment, there was an element of danger and discovery in their tryst—one that was impishly adolescent, and thrilling, freeing. She felt impossibly young, and just as

vulnerable. Ross seemed even more sensually determined now than earlier, and for the first time
seemed to need something from her. Could it be her
devotion, her love?

"Are you afraid of what others will think?" Both
of his hands framed her face, his fingertips sliding
back through the silky masses of her hair. His
mouth hovered lower, resting just the barest distance above her own.

Her eyes closed. "No, I'm not afraid." She drifted
in the delightful sensations. "And of course I want
to be with you." If Teddy had not been there to
chaperon their initial meeting that evening....

He grinned, cajoling teasingly, his fragrant breath
whispering across her face. "Ah, a woman after my
own heart..." he teased lightly.

"Precisely the problem," she bantered in return,
loving the hazy cocoon of love their closeness generated. "Around you, I don't seem to have any idea of
what constitutes proper behavior." Her fingertips
did a lazy tap dance over his shoulders, his chest and
drifted on downward to his waist. He shuddered vo-
luptuously in response, his thighs tautening against
hers.

"You don't need an etiquette book to tell you what
you feel," he said with gruff impatience. "And God
knows I want you, have since the first moment I set
eyes on you this evening, tripping quickly down the
stairs, your hair flying around your face, your
cheeks full of agitated color." He drew back, his
brows lowering, giving serious emphasis to his
words. "The errand was more than a nice gesture on
my part or an excuse to get you a gift—and for the
record I *was* planning to take Teddy to the sporting-
goods store just as soon as the opportunity pre-
sented itself. It was survival. Had I stayed...." He

didn't finish the thoughts with words, but showed her what would have been had they not been blessed with a nine-year-old chaperon.

His mouth fitted to hers, filling her to overflowing with a fiery tumescence. It was a firm, deliberate kiss, an act of total male domination, a result of pent-up emotions from several days of separation and unexpressed longing on both their parts. His weight bore down against hers, molding her to him ardently, crushing her against both him and the hard metal of the Jeep. It was an excruciatingly wonderful pressure. His need was a palpable force, more dangerously seductive even than the seeking, ever deepening quality of his kiss. His hands tangled in her hair, slid over her shoulders to her spine. She succumbed completely, wanting and needing him so very badly, barely aware of the crowds of people on the other side of the trees separating park and parking lot. Abruptly, Ross lifted his head, gazing down at her, as if only just realizing what he had been about to do. "Eileen—"

He did need her, she realized with a start, as desperately as she needed him. And in that instant she would have surrendered her very soul to him because she knew with total certainty that she was in love with him, deeply, irrevocably, in love. "Don't stop," she said softly. "Not just yet...."

He groaned deep and low in his throat, pleasure suffusing her as she ignored the low, loving growl and instead laced her hands enticingly around his nape. Ever so slowly, his head bent and his mouth possessed hers again, tantalizing, taking, inviting further pleasure and evoking a whirlwind of emotion. She was enveloped in the clean musky scent of him, the unique taste and texture of his mouth. His hand moved beneath the hem of her sweater to lightly stroke the bare skin of her back. Palm splayed against her skin, he held her passionately close until every cell in her body was riotously aflame. When the kiss finally ended several ragged moments later, both were stunned, silent, strangely content, yet physically aching. "I'm falling in love with you," he said softly. "You know that."

"Yes. I'm falling in love with you, too." All they needed now to make their loving unit complete was Teddy's approval, and she sensed they already had that. Wordlessly, Ross stalked around to remove the promised wrap from his Jeep. He tossed her the sweatshirt, smiling briefly at her quick responses when she caught it.

"Hopefully, this will keep you warm enough," he remarked huskily, casting a reluctant glance toward the park as if sorry they had to go back to eat with the others. But Teddy was not someone either of them would willingly let down.

She flushed, obediently pulling the bulky gray-and-blue material, emblazoned with the Running Tigers and Jake's Hardware store insignias, over her head. Inadvertently in the process her sweater rode up, baring her midriff to his view. Ross put a hand up to capture the cloth, his hand lightly tracing her skin, preventing her from further immodesty. "Thanks," she murmured hoarsely.

"I don't want you to freeze," he said gently. "Though I guess by now it's obvious that this was the least of my motives for bringing you out here. I wanted to say a *real* hello." He took a deep bolstering breath. "And if we don't get back to the others soon, I'll be tempted to do it again and again and again."

There was nothing Eileen would have liked better than to bring him home and directly into her bed. "We'll have time alone together," she promised.

Ross nodded. "We'll make time."

They both looked ridiculously happy when they returned to the others. Janey said, in an aside as they were lining up to eat, "See what I told you? That romantic gleam!"

Eileen couldn't have agreed more.

Ross spent most of the dinner hour entertaining Teddy and urging him to eat all of his vegetables as well as his meat. Eileen enjoyed their banter, but was in reality only half there, for wearing Ross's sweatshirt was like drowning in the scent of his cologne and skin. Unable to help herself, she fantasized endlessly about him during the cookout, remembering the pleasant interlude on her patio, on her sofa, the earlier kiss near his Jeep. How she wished they could be together that very night!

Later, after cleanup was finally over, Hugh wandered over to inform them casually, "*Revenge of the Swamp Monster* is on the late show tonight." Then he said, "I know this is short notice, but uh, would you mind if Teddy spent the night? I kind of half promised the boys they could watch it together."

Eileen surveyed Hugh's sheepish expression. It was clear Janey had put him up to another matchmaking ploy. She could have hugged her in gratitude and delight! Cautiously, she said, "You're sure you don't mind?" Teddy was over at the Deverauxes a lot.

Hugh shrugged off the inconvenience nonchalantly. "It will do them good to be together. And besides," Hugh added, as Janey joined them, "I cut the grass first thing tomorrow morning. I could use an extra hand with the trimming and sweeping. After that, we'll go swimming. You can pick him up any time you want."

"Is noon okay?" she asked, her eyes aglow.

"Fine," Hugh and Janey chorused.

"Thank you," Ross graciously added. "Eileen and I will return the favor and take the children out sometime so the two of you can go out."

"Great!" exclaimed an enthusiastic Janey, as Hugh grinned his agreement.

Teddy obediently gave Eileen a kiss, and the boys departed, promising between giggles to be good. Ross drove her home then carried the picnic hamper and dishes into her kitchen. "Can I fix you some coffee?" Eileen asked softly. Now that they were alone, she was becoming somewhat nervous.

"Please." Ross smiled in understanding.

When she joined him in the living room several minutes later, she had removed the borrowed sweatshirt and run a brush through her hair. Ross, his feet propped up on a footstool was engrossed in the evening paper. Seeing her, he quickly put the paper aside, granting her his full attention. It was a cozy domestic scene, a premonition of what could be between them with luck. Eileen put the tray down on the table and poured Ross a steaming cup of coffee. As she handed him the saucer, she recalled what Janey had told her. Softly, she said, "Thank you for being so understanding about my work this evening."

He sighed, then admitted with disarming honesty, his eyes meeting hers, "There was a time when I wouldn't have been. I like to think I've changed since then. I hope I have." Without Teddy's rambunctious presence, the living room seemed oddly silent. Suddenly there was so much more she needed to know about him. "Why is it you never talk about your son or your ex-wife?" she asked. He knew everything about her first marriage. She knew nothing about his.

"It's a long, very unhappy story." He shrugged. "I didn't want to bore you."

She flushed, holding her coffee cup before her like a shield. "I just wanted you to know I'm here for you, the same way that you are for me."

"I know that," he said gently. "And it means a lot to me, more than you know. Having a woman as lovely and talented as you in my corner isn't something I would ever take for granted. Nor do I mean to shut you out." He took a sip of coffee, finally continuing in a matter-of-fact tone, "The breakup of my marriage isn't easy for me to talk about even now, primarily because in the course of the divorce I inadvertently lost several precious years with my son that can never be regained. That hurts. I also didn't want you to think I was giving you the old my-first-wife-never-understood-me line, in an effort to score points. Thus, the less said on the subject the better." He laughed mirthlessly, and it was a harsh bitter sound, a testament to how deeply he had been hurt.

"What's worse is that the reasons we divorced are almost a cliché these days. They weren't then. Arielle left me to find herself. She said I stifled her... creatively, intellectually, emotionally. You name it, her complaints ran the gamut." He shrugged bewilderedly. Knowing how gentle and compassionate a man Ross was, Eileen understood his incomprehension of his ex-wife's attitude.

Ross continued, "I don't know. She was an artist, and by her standards maybe I am too straightlaced. It's true I wanted a relatively standard life with family, kids, a home in the country, pets, the works. She wanted endless vistas and the freedom to come and go as she chose. She also wanted money and I didn't have nearly enough, not for the sophisticated

jet-setting kind of life she wanted to be able to lead.
So eventually she left me and took my son with her.
She knew I would've fought her for custody, had she
approached me about a divorce at that point. Because she was also unfaithful, as I later discovered, I
probably would have won. So she just took off, saying she was living with friends for a few weeks to
think everything through. When she returned, we
would try to work out our problems together. Like a
fool, I agreed. Oh, I had my misgivings about her
taking Stephen with her, but I also knew how much
she loved him. So I let her go. By the time I discovered what she'd really done, it was too late. She
didn't even leave me a note, nothing—she just disappeared. I lost track of them both for several years.
It was the worst period of my life. Meanwhile, I
worked night and day to build my firm. I went
through a lot of women, and I wasn't necessarily
very kind to them, although I was never deliberately
cruel. They just didn't matter to me."

That much Eileen understood. When Ted had
died, she'd resented other men. Oh, she'd dated now
and then, but never with the intention of getting involved. She'd wanted to play it safe, to keep from
getting hurt. Only with Ross had she begun to open
up again to the possibilities of love.

Sighing, he continud, "Finally, through the help
of a private detective, I tracked Arielle to the Carib-
bean. She was planning to marry a wealthy English-
man and wanted a divorce. By then, my son barely
remembered me, so total custody was out of the
question. Finally, we hammered out a deal that was
in Steve's best interests. Now I see Stephen four
times a year. Twice I visit him, and he comes to see
me over the Thanksgiving holidays and spring vacation. In between, we call each other on the phone

and write letters, but it's not the same. It's not the kind of relationship I ever envisioned us having." He sighed, suddenly looking much older than his thirty-five years.

The loss of his son seemed his largest regret. Yet she had to know, had to ask if there was more to his pain than he was letting on. "Are you still in love with Arielle?"

"No." He looked at her steadily. "I'm not sure I ever really was. She claims I never saw her for what she was, and in retrospect I see she was right. We were married straight out of college, just before I started law school. She got pregnant almost right away. It was an unplanned, difficult pregnancy. Her initial dismay aside, however, she was an excellent mother. Timewise, I was very pressured at that stage in my life, and as a result I wasn't much of a husband or father. Because of our financial situation, Arielle worked part-time in a crafts shop. That cut into her time at the easel drastically, and she became very frustrated and resentful, especially of me, because I was essentially doing what I wanted to do in life. She wasn't."

He rose and paced the room, gesturing as he talked. "When she tried to tell me how she felt, I insisted it would get better, given time and the improvement of our financial situation, which I was working like hell to correct." He sighed, pivoting toward Eileen. "I see now how naive I was, but I really believed that at the time. By the time Stephen was six, she was fed up with my long hours away from home, the pressure upon me to pass the boards and later to do well in court. Finally, she didn't even try to talk to me—just packed her bags and walked out, taking Stevie with her."

Eileen set her cup aside and smoothed the crease

in her slacks. "Would you have listened if she had come to you?"

"Now, yes. Then, not as well. Some lessons come hard."

"I know." She thought of her own life with Ted, the blind spots she'd had. She'd failed to see the danger signals coming from her own husband. Maybe, like Ross, she just hadn't wanted to see, had been afraid to see. Both she and Ross had been so young and scared, at the same time dealing with the awesome responsibility of a child. Yet, they'd both wanted their marriages to work.

Ross finally came back to sit down beside her on the sofa. She knew now how much he'd been hurt. "I'm sorry about your son," she murmured sympathetically, clasping his left hand with her own, "and that you don't have more time together. Have you talked to your wife about the possibility of split custody?"

"She feels Stephen is hers, that she raised him from the beginning. Initially, of course, I would have taken her to court. That's why she fled the country. Now, it wouldn't be fair to him to uproot him. And it's Stephen's welfare I'm concerned most about, not my own."

Eileen knew that feeling well. In the years since Ted's death she had sacrificed much for her son. And there were times, even now, when it still seemed like not nearly enough. She turned toward Ross, her palms resting lightly on his forearms. He read the desire in her eyes. He shook his head slowly. "No, Eileen, this is the wrong reason to be intimate."

"Please, Ross, just let me hold you."

She moved closer, wanting so much to ease his pain and continue what they had started earlier in the evening. He capitulated with a groan, his arms encircling her back. The next instant they were reclining on the sofa. Tenderly, he leaned over her, his weight braced on his forearms, positioned on either side of her head. He paused to find a pillow and cushion it comfortably beneath her neck. His eyes roamed her freely, studying the tousled disarray of her hair, the parted lips, the flushed cheeks. "God, you're lovely," he murmured, "so sweet. And in this one respect, so naive. I don't think you have any idea what you do to me."

She didn't feel naive. She felt wanton and warm and more in love than she'd ever dreamed possible. "Kiss me," she whispered, teasing him in a husky voice, spurred on by the disbelieving look on his face. "And we'll see who's naive."

He indulged her whim, his lips possessively claiming hers. Their tongues mingled, the kiss drawing out languorously. He moved back, but she caught his head bringing it close to hers. Her teeth raked his tongue, catching it with gentle pressure, while her fingertips trailed through his hair. Her love for him, newly blossomed and discovered, made her bold. Her fingertips trailed lower to the hem of his shirt. She delighted at the look of amazement in his eyes as she slid her palms beneath the navy fabric. She touched the hard sinews of his back, his more heavily muscled chest. As Eileen's fingers moved upward they captured the masculine nipples and crossed over to touch Ross's bony sternum. He gasped as she raked her fingernails lightly into his belly, trailing ever downward to the silky line that disappeared into the line of his jeans. He shifted against her, impatient, warm and hard.

"You know what you're asking to happen." His breathing was ragged. There was a faint sheen of perspiration beading his upper lip. Yet for the moment, he was still in complete control.

Eileen pulled her palms from beneath his shirt and traced the hard, angular lines of his jaw. Yes, she knew what she was doing. She swallowed hard, taking a deep, shaky breath. "I want you to make love to me," she whispered, caressing him persuasively, passionately, as she spoke. "I want to make love to you." Unbeknownst to him, she'd seen a doctor a few days prior and prepared herself for protection.

He stared down at her, threading his fingers through her hair. "Why tonight?" he said softly. There was a new tension in his voice, an untrusting light in his eyes.

Because I love you, she thought. But suddenly the words wouldn't come for fear of scaring him away, fear he wouldn't feel quite as intensely, especially after all he had told her. She dropped her gaze shyly, stared intently at the hair rising from the open placket of his shirt. Would the rest of him be as exquisite to touch, too? Could she ever forget the way he had looked, naked, outside the cabana? Finally, she said, "You've had to sacrifice so much for your son, Ross. I've sacrificed nearly as much for Teddy, though in different ways. It isn't fair for us to have to go through the rest of our lives alone. We shouldn't have to give this up, too."

Too late, she realized how pragmatic her reasoning sounded. He sat up abruptly, swinging his legs over the side of the couch. When she didn't immediately follow, he grasped her hand and pulled her up to a sitting position. "I see," he said roughly, all passion gone. "Kind of like a support system for single suffering parents. I don't want you out of pity, Eileen. Not tonight, not ever."

"That's not what I meant!" She followed his long

angry strides to the door, panic nearly overwhelming her. Why had she ever brought that up? Why hadn't she left well enough alone?

He paused, his fists clenching with the effort it was taking not to touch her. The timing was all wrong for other reasons, too. The bitterness from his failed marriage had intruded upon their bliss. "You don't know how I wish I could believe that," he swore softly.

She didn't want to pursue him in his current mood, but neither could she just let him go, knowing he was hurting. She wanted to help him as he had helped her. "It's true," she said softly. She reached out for him, but he held her off with the upraised palm of his hand. The agony of his physical frustration was reflected in every movement.

"Tell that to me tomorrow," he said tightly, "and maybe, just maybe, I'll believe it. But tonight, God help me, I'm going to do the right thing." Without a backward glance, he strode out her door and down the walk to his car. She stayed there, framed in the doorway until he'd driven away. Eileen closed the door slowly. She waited up for nearly an hour, hoping he would change his mind, call or come back to talk it out. He didn't.

Finally, switching off the lights, she went slowly up to bed. Sleep was a long time coming. Her dreams were filled with Ross's face. She ached for his kiss, his touch. She woke, just short of fulfillment, calling his name.

7

It seemed to Eileen only minutes later that a sharp, ringing sound penetrated the pleasant lethargy filling her sleep-hazed mind. *Go away*, she thought irascibly. *Saturday's my day to sleep late!* The shrill noise continued. Groggily, she groped for the receiver, inadvertently knocking over the alarm clock, two books and a pad and pencil before stilling the noisy invention. *It better be good*, she thought, lifting the receiver to her ear. Her hello sounded like a muffled harumpf. There was a lengthy pause. "Eileen?" a male voice drawled with soft hesitation. "Did I wake you?"

Ross! Eileen sat bolt upright in bed, every cell of her absolutely awake. Early-morning sunlight streamed through the draperied windows, illuminating her bedroom in a halo of gold. Propping herself up on an elbow she held the blue princess phone to her ear. "I hate to admit it, but yes, you did wake me." With effort, she matched his well-modulated perky tone and squinted at the clock, raking a hand through her hair. "What time is it?" She tried but failed to stifle a yawn.

He chuckled deep in his throat. "Nine-thirty."

Eileen groaned. She hadn't slept so deeply in ages. Part of it, she knew, was due to the emotional exhaustion from the past tumultuous week. The other half was prompted by the roller-coaster sensation of falling in love with Ross Mitchell, and the fact that before she'd finally drifted off she'd been up half the night thinking about him and his unexpected refusal of her sensual invitation.

"About last night," she began shyly.

"I'm the one who's sorry. I left rather abruptly," he admitted penitently.

Curling her fingers around the telephone cord, she continued, "I did feel a lot of empathy for what you had been through, losing daily access to your son. I don't know what I'd ever do without Teddy. I couldn't have managed the past decade if I hadn't had him to love and care about. But that wasn't why I wanted us to be together, Ross."

"I know that," he admitted softly. "But I had to be sure. That's why I didn't call or come back later, after I'd thought it over. I felt we both needed time to think."

"Well, sport—" she used his favorite pet name with affection "—you were in my dreams all last night."

He laughed. "And you were in mine."

"So what are we going to do about it?" she asked, glad to hear the lightness back in his voice.

He continued pleasantly, "That's why I'm calling—to ask you to be my date for the Man of the Year dinner. I know Janey mentioned it to you. What do you say?" He gave her no time to refuse. "Shall I pick you up at seven? It's black tie."

"That'll be fine." An unreasonable joy buoyed Eileen. "I'm glad." She needed him with her.

His sigh reverberated shakily in her ear. "I'll see you soon then."

He arrived promptly at seven, but Eileen was still dressing—this time minus Teddy's badgering. She had selected a misty pink chiffon dress that bared her shoulders. Its tight-fitting bodice hugged her breasts and waist and flared out to fullness around her hips. The full skirt whispered enticingly when she walked. A ruffled flounce across the bodice added a softly feminine touch to an otherwise classically designed dress.

Adjusting the straps on her pale-pink satin sandals, Eileen started down the stairs. Ross rose when he saw her, and his look of admiration tightened her throat.

Mrs. Quan, Teddy's sitter, was knitting in a nearby chair. She looked up and smiled. "Mrs. Garrett, you do look lovely."

"I'll second that," Ross agreed in a husky voice.

She turned her gaze to his and clutched his hand. "Thank you." She knelt to give Teddy a brief hug. "You be good for Mrs. Quan, now. Bedtime is promptly at nine-thirty."

"What happens if I'm watching an hour-long show?" he asked.

"It's still nine-thirty." She remained firm.

"Okay." He went unconcernedly back to watching television. The many extracurricular events of the past two days had worn him out. Swiftly, Eileen instructed Mrs. Quan as to where they could be reached. Then, Ross led her out to the car, helping her settle inside without crushing her dress. As he slid in behind the wheel, he added again, "I meant what I said. You do look lovely."

A rush of pleasure swept through her. Ross was a very successful, private, intense man, and she was drawn as much to his tenderness as to his strength. But sitting beside him, all she could think about was how his lips felt tracing patterns on her skin, and the shatteringly erotic variations of his kiss. "You look devastating in black tie," she murmured.

The white pleated shirt accented the tan of his skin, and his hair was neatly brushed, dark against the exquisitely tailored silk suit. Fitting the key into the ignition, he looked as glamorous as a male model and perfectly at ease.

He reached for her, tracing the line of her cheekbone with his knuckle in one velvet sweep. "I'm glad you're going to be with me tonight." Ross stroked the underside of her chin, tantalizing her to an almost unbearable degree. "There's no other woman I'd want by my side on such an important night. In fact, until I met you I was planning to go stag."

"I'm glad you asked me."

Janey and Hugh met them at the hotel ballroom civic center. Ross was seated front and center on the dais. He touched her continually through the evening, his hand clasping hers with quiet possessiveness at every available opportunity, his knee brushing her thigh beneath the table. It was as if, she thought in a heady whirlwind of delight, he wanted everyone there to know she was his woman. More surprising still was the knowledge she wanted to be his lover. She wanted to know him as intimately as it was possible to know another human being, and she wanted him to love her in that way, too. The misery she had felt with Ted had dimmed to a blur in her past. She wanted the present, and she wanted it more than anything she had ever yearned for.

After a dinner of chauteaubriand and champagne, the awards were given. Ross's citation, the most important, was given last. Hands folded on her lap, tears of emotion glistening in her eyes, Eileen listened proudly as he was cited for his work with the softball league, the local men's organization and his many hours devoted to law enforcement and urban renewal, often at little or no charge. Concluding, the master of ceremonies remarked, "Our fair city would not be nearly as bright, were it not for the continued efforts of this man. Ross Mitchell, we now officially declare you our Man of the Year."

Thunderous applause sounded as Ross took his place at the podium. Watching him confidently delivering his acceptance speech, Eileen felt as if her heart were bursting with happiness. As he concluded his speech, Ross accepted the award with gratitude, giving credit to all those who had made his efforts more effective. Eileen's eyes were shimmering with tears when he sat down beside her. He squeezed her hand, simultaneously amused and touched by her emotional display. "I wasn't that great a speaker!" he teased.

"But you are a very dynamic man." She felt fortunate to know him, fortunate to be his date.

He lifted his glass of champagne in adoring salute. "If ever there was a woman capable of taming me, lady, it's you."

Ross stood and shook hands with several men and women before whisking her onto the dance floor and holding her against his hard, lean strength. The warm hand encircling her back prompted her closer. Leaning down to whisper in her ear, he murmured softly as the other dancers spun by, a disjointed shimmer of gaiety, movement and music. She was aware only of him, and he of her.

He folded her close, his thighs nudging hers. Her arms wreathed his neck, and she shifted closer, her breasts pressing against the thin fabric of her dress. His eyes darkened as her flesh transmitted warmth to his. She felt the stirrings of his desire. Minutes passed. The liquid sway of their communing thighs emphasized the desires burning within them, like wildfire touched to dry tinder. "Let's get out of here," he said finally, covering her with an ardent gaze, which promised to deliver as much as it demanded. And she knew instinctively Ross Mitchell was a man who would demand a lot. His voice was a husky murmur. "I want to spend some time alone with you."

"Your place?" Her heart seemed to be pounding in her throat.

He nodded. "If you're sure."

"I am. More than ever."

He lived in a wooded section north of town, his house hidden by a wealth of pine, maple and walnut trees. It was a traditional red brick Cape Cod, beautifully designed and carefully maintained, the shutters and doors painted a smooth glossy black. Inside, the decor was elegant but comfortable, in subtle shades of off-white and gunmetal gray. Within minutes, he had champagne chilling in a silver ice bucket on the coffee table. He plucked a flower from the vase and threaded it through her hair, his fingertips gently massaging the silken mass. "I like your hair like that, all loose and flowing," he murmured with an appreciative glance.

Now that they were there, alone, he seemed to be in no rush. She began to relax. He left the room easily and came back with a velvet-lined box. Eileen stared at it wonderingly. With a generous smile, he placed it in her hands. "Go on, open it," he said. "Please."

With trembling fingers, she undid the catch. Inside, against the glitter of dark-blue velvet were delicate earrings, each eighteen-carat-gold piece hand crafted in the shape of a fallen oak leaf, studded with tiny diamonds. They bore a remarkably close resemblance to the pair of earrings she had lost. For the second time that evening, she was overwhelmed with emotion. She blinked rapidly to stall off tears of happiness. "Oh, Ross, they're lovely—thank you!"

"You like them?" he asked anxiously, watching her closely.

"Yes. Oh, yes." She sat stunned, cradling the jewelry box in her hands. The earrings were breathtakingly beautiful. Wordlessly, he removed an earring from the case. With deft easy strokes, he was already unhooking the gold-braided hoops she wore in her earlobes. Ever so gently, he threaded the new leaf-shaped adornment in her ear, then had her turn so he could remove and then fasten the other.

When he had finished, Ross put some soft music on the stereo and drew her down beside him. She sat turned across his lap, her head braced on his shoulder, his arm clamped around her waist. The flat of his palm cozily encircled her ribs, splayed fingertips resting just below the full swelling curve of her breasts. "To us," he toasted intimately.

"To us," she said throatily, sipping her champagne. *And to love. May this moment continue forever.* The bubbles tickled her nose. Sweet golden liquor sped through her veins.

His mouth lingered at her temple, then followed the curve of her cheekbone to her mouth. Champagne and passion were on their lips. Then his mouth followed the slender line of her shoulder, gliding across the bare skin above the low neckline of her dress.

"I want you," he confessed raggedly, lifting his head. His mouth covered hers with a deep hungry kiss that left her shaken.

"And I want to be with you," she admitted, "so very much." He drew her to her feet and gently removed the glass of champagne from her hand.

"Then let's go upstairs." He led her to his bedroom. It was most definitely a man's lair, Eileen noted, with a king-size bed, draped in softest midnight-blue velvet. The deep-pile carpeting in a harmonizing lighter hue bespoke taste and style. A stereo and elaborate video cassette recorder occupied a bookshelf opposite the bed. Outside the French doors, a wood deck overlooked the forested property. The adjacent bath was fully equipped with a clear-glass shower stall and separate marble tub. Suddenly, she was overwhelmed and more than a little bit nervous. It had been so long since she'd actually been with a man.

Sensing this, Ross selected a tape and plugged it into the stereo. Low, soothing music filled the room, setting an intimate mood. "We have as much time as you need," he said softly, reassuringly. Never taking his eyes from her, he loosened his tie, unbuttoned his coat... the first several fastenings of his shirt.

Watching, Eileen wet her lips with her tongue. She worried suddenly about the tiny white lines marking her hips that had appeared with Teddy's birth, now nearly invisible. Would Ross notice she was not exactly a nineteen-year-old, perfect in every respect?

His hands stroked the length of her arms, lingering at the width of her shoulders, then moving to gently caress her throat. "Tell me you're not trembling because you're afraid of me," he said softly.

"Not afraid, just nervous." Suddenly, she was terribly insecure.

His eyes swept over her in a yearning, adoring gesture. He caught her hand, held it tightly, and brought it to his lips. "Oh God, Eileen." A shudder swept through him. "Don't you know how desirable you are to me? What sweet torture it's been to be near you all these days and not undress you swiftly, rush you into bed and make love to you? I cherish the time we have together. And if anyone's worried about not being perfect...."

"You're perfect to me, too." Needing him so, sure they were meant to be together, she laced her arms around his neck. Very deliberately he gazed down at her and then lowered his lips to brush hers. She stood on tiptoe, moving nearer, kissing him back. He capitulated with a groan, and the caresses that followed were a soul-stirring, dizzying kaleidoscope of pleasure. "Better?" he asked long moments later as she relaxed against him.

She favored him with a crooked half-smile, returning the silly badinage. "All systems go and ready for take-off."

He grinned back, just as devilishly. "Not yet," he said easily, his eyes dark with sweet, tender promise. "But soon. May I?" He touched the back zipper of her dress.

Lowering her eyes shyly, Eileen nodded. Turning her around, Ross unfastened the zipper of her dress. Chill air assaulted her skin as the edges of cloth were parted. She heard his intake of breath as he discovered she was braless. The cut of the dress wouldn't allow one, hence support had been sewn into the silken lining. As the fabric fell away slowly, her pink-tipped breasts met his appreciative gaze. His hands circled round her, cupped the swelling orbs, burning the sensitive tips. He drew her back against him until her head rested against his shoulder, the vapor of his breath tantalizing her face. "I've been wanting to do this all night," he whispered, measuring and lifting the plump weight. "You have such touchable skin, soft and ripe."

Ripe. Like the woman she had become and, because of circumstance, had yet to fully discover. She turned toward him, needing for a moment the security of his arms. He held her for long moments, his hand soothing the skin of her back. She followed his lead, her touch teasing and tender and curious. The rest of her dress was peeled off. The stiff fabric rustled as she stepped out of the floor-length garment. Eileen bent before him to remove her high-heeled sandals. Fascinated, he steadied her with one hand, and then carefully peeled off her glittery pale-pink panty hose, until all that remained were her lacy white bikini panties. She was nearly naked, and he was still fully dressed.

"Unfair, Ross, this will never do." Eileen helped him out of his jacket and tie. Once his cummerbund was removed, the buttons on his shirt were quickly opened. He drew her down onto the bed, his fingertips beginning a magic glide over her skin. "Sweet," he whispered, "so sweet." The last barrier of cloth was removed. He stripped down swiftly to complete vulnerability, a modern-day Adonis with trim waist, firm buttocks and thighs, then joined her on the bed. His legs entwined with hers. He slid lower, his palms covering her breasts. She felt sweet pressure, the plucking motion of his splayed fingertips tantalizing the pebble-hard tips. A purr sounded deep in her throat. She arched against him, needing more intimate contact, wanting to touch skin to skin. Holding her firmly, his lips and tongue bathed the sensitized nipples. Desire inside her blossomed, grew to an unbearable level, inciting her to further boldness, the brazen invitation to make love. Eileen's heart hammered inside her chest as one wandering palm slid lower. His other hand slid beneath her, arching her spine up and against him as his other hand further opened her thighs. "Ross," she groaned out her frustration.

"I love you, Eileen," he murmured passionately. She loved the feel of his hands on her skin. "I never thought I'd feel this strongly."

It was precisely what she needed to demolish the last barriers of wariness and modesty between them. She gloried in the knowledge that they shared this discovery of love, the night of fulfillment and pleasure. He stroked lightly, swiftly, then slowly, more intimately, searching out each feminine fold of silken pink flesh like an explorer on a timeless voyage. There were no barriers, nothing sacred, nothing denied. It seemed natural and right for her to touch him in the same way. She arched against him, murmuring frenzied cries. He caught her to him and moved upward, his leg sliding between hers as he tenderly whispered her name. "Yes," he urged softly. "Please. Hold me like that, Eileen. Touch me... yes, my love...that's it...yes, sweetheart, yes...."

Following the decisive molding of his palms, she curved her spine, arching her pelvis upward into his. Their bodies fully touching, she wreathed her arms around his neck, then seconds later slid frantically lower to dig impatiently, passionately into the base of his spine. Without warning his hands swept between them, parting their bodies deliberately, unexpectedly, and he caressed her lightly from collarbone to thigh. He was delaying what she wanted and needed from him, prolonging and heightening their pleasure. Yet still he denied them that sweet anguish, taking his time, orchestrating her every sensation, his every pulsing move. Until finally there was no more holding back, no more delaying, only the swift sure movements of his body over hers as he possessed her finally and forever, the wild sweetness humming in her veins, the sensation of being joined heart and soul, forever. And ever and ever....

It seemed aeons before they tumbled mystically

back to earth. Her heart slowed only marginally. The sweet physical contentment was surpassed only by the glowing feeling inside her. She felt cherished, as if for the first time in her life she had really been loved by a man.

"I could stay here forever," Eileen murmured drowsily at last. Limbs entwined, her head on his chest, his hand absentmindedly stroking her hair, they lay cradled together.

Ross snuggled closer, wrapping her securely in the protective curve of his strong arms. "Comfortable, hmm?" He sounded lazy, filled with love.

"I feel as if I'm in seventh heaven," she murmured, casting him a shy look. "How about you?" She pressed another kiss across his steadily thrumming heart, loving the salty unique taste of his skin. Her fingers threaded possessively through the mat of hair on his chest.

"Better. Like I'm floating on air. Like I've been granted the realization of my most magnificent dream."

"Does that mean I was all right?" She giggled at the sheer adoration in his eyes.

He turned swiftly, rolling her onto her back, so that she lay beneath him once again. "Lady," he said, taking her lips once again and teasing them apart with his, "you were fabulous...."

"Yes," Eileen said on a sigh, stroking his arms, then his thighs with renewed vigor and exuberance. "Yes...yes...yes...."

Finally, however, time and reality intruded once again. Nothing in this life came free, Eileen thought ruefully, including a moment in sheer heaven. A dutiful glance at the clock informed her it was well after midnight. Sadly, she had to go. "Ross?" Her voice was husky with endearment as she searched the floor for her clothes. "I've got to get my sitter home." Mrs. Quan would be wondering where Eileen was. Though she said she'd be late, she couldn't delay much longer.

Ross jerked around toward the steadily ticking timekeeper. He'd been lazily caressing her hip. Now he sat up, a rueful expression on his face. "I'd almost forgotten you have to go." Stretching, he reluctantly swung his legs over the edge of the bed. Her eyes were drawn to the superbly muscled skin of his back. His voice was husky with sleep and contentment with what they had shared. His wistful glance showed that, like her, he wished their moment in time could last forever.

"We're going to have to work this out so we can spend the entire night together, soon," he said.

"I agree." There wasn't anything she wanted more. "But for the moment—"

He laughed softly. "I know, Cinderella." Stifling a contented yawn behind the back of his hand, he rummaged around the room for his tux. "I've got to spirit you back home to your castle."

Their good-night at her apartment was necessarily chaste. As she undressed for bed, she felt a special glow, the satisfaction of a contented woman. Nothing had ever felt so right.

THE NEXT MONTH PASSED in a dizzying haze. The Running Tigers played in ten softball games, eight of which they won. Teddy adapted to the routine of practice with amazing ease. And win or lose, his mood was gregariously chipper. Ross was thoughtful and attentive, seeing Eileen whenever possible for lunch, taking her and Teddy to the movies or out to dinner. And as days passed they became more and more a blended family unit. The three of them attended a nearby county fair and discussed the possibility of seeing a play together later in the summer.

The last weekend in July, they took both Brian and Teddy out to the lake for a picnic. Afterward, the boys tossed a Frisbee around the grass. Ross reclined next to Eileen, watching them contentedly. "I don't know when I've ever been so happy," he confided, one eye on the boys. As he turned back to her, his fingers twined in a strand of her hair. His gaze roamed her face as if he were memorizing every plane, contemplating how best to kiss or caress every inch of her.

She shifted restlessly on the blanket beside him. Beneath the placid Sunday-afternoon atmosphere, sexual frustration simmered. "I wish we had more time alone together," she admitted restlessly. She was beginning to realize she wanted more out of life than an occasional hour or so in his bed. Because of her son, she and Ross had managed only a few hurried trysts at his place.

"I want to be with you more, too." She was suddenly aware of all of him, the hardness of his thighs, the gentleness of his touch, the way he had of looking at her so intensely her breath stopped.

"Do you think it's possible we could get away together?" he asked, his eyes caressing the soft disarray of her hair and the swell of her breasts beneath the thin teal-blue camp shirt. His fingertip drew a line down the crease of her white cotton shorts. Her skin began to prickle with increasing heat. "Just the two of us?"

Her heart soared with the possibility. She basked in the scent of his cologne, brisk and disturbingly male.

"Teddy is going to visit my parents next week."

"How long will he be gone?" His eyes darkened as he mentally ran through the possibilities.

"Two weeks. I drive him up on Saturday and return Sunday." She could work the whole time. They'd have every night. If Ross wanted it that way, of course.

Ross stared at Teddy and Brian for a long while. After a moment he turned back to her. His expression was as serious as she had ever seen it. "Could you get out of town for a week or so?"

"I've got time off coming from work." She looked up into his enigmatic turquoise eyes. Her heart was pounding somewhere near her throat.

"I've rented a place in Bermuda. I go there every year." His voice was a rough seductive whisper, but his words carried the emotional ramifications of a serious involvement. "I'd like you to meet my son."

Her heart soared. She knew how important a step this was—for Ross and for her. "I'd like that, too."

She didn't have a lot of extra money to work with, but if she dug into some of her savings she could scrape up the necessary amount.

THE WEEK PASSED in a flurry of activity. The day before Teddy and Eileen were to leave for her parents' farm, Ross called and said he would like to take Teddy fishing on a friend's boat.

"It'll be sort of a farewell party for the three of us. I'll meet you both at your place at five-thirty."

Cheerfully, Eileen packed a picnic dinner for the three of them. Ross promised to supply the equipment and sportsman's expertise.

The appointed time arrived. Teddy was in rare form, dancing back and forth, clearly even more excited than he had been the night of the Little League family picnic at the park. He was wearing his Running Tigers practice jersey and jeans. His baseball cap was slightly askew on his head. To her mild exasperation, every five minutes he asked what time it was and when Ross would be coming. When six-thirty had come and gone, with no Ross, she began to get worried. Finally Eileen called the office and discovered Ross and Lenoir Collins, his firm's new junior partner, had both been called to Chicago on a business emergency. He phoned from O'Hare airport later that evening. "Eileen, I'm sorry. Did my office get in touch with you?"

Her tone was icy to cover her hurt. "I called them. They told me."

He swore curtly at the mix-up, then sighed. "I'm sorry. I asked my secretary to call you right away. I was tied up on long distance. By the time I got off the phone it was time to leave for the airport, and I had no time to get to a phone before boarding the plane." He sighed, concluding, "We've got a major problem here with one of my clients. It could turn into a class-action suit if we don't do some successful negotiating over the next twenty-four hours. Frankly, I don't know when I'll be back at this point. Forgive me?" *Easier said than done,* Eileen thought, observing the crestfallen look on her son's face as he realized from the tone of the conversation that Ross wasn't going to put in an appearance at all. "Tell Teddy I'll make it up to him?" Ross coaxed in a much gentler tone.

At the sound of his voice, so velvety sure, her knees weakened. "Sure." But deep inside she was stiff with resentment. This was all too reminiscent of the many times her husband had let her down. And she had promised herself Teddy would never go through the same, not with anyone.

Ross urged quietly, "Put Teddy on the phone."

Only because she knew Teddy wouldn't be able to sleep until he had talked to his "pal," did Eileen manage to pleasantly hand over the receiver to her son. Ross talked to Teddy for a good ten minutes, at the end of which Teddy, too, was only slightly mollified. *Like mother, like son,* she thought. *Neither of us bears disappointment well.* At her direction, Teddy stomped out to the kitchen for a glass of milk and a cookie while Eileen talked to Ross.

"I'll make this up to him, I promise," Ross said tensely.

"I know," she assured him. But in her heart, Eileen wasn't sure. She felt, in some respects, as if Ross had begun taking her for granted. And it wasn't a feeling she liked or wanted to encourage.

He paused. "Tell me you understand." The entreaty was soft, pleading.

But she couldn't, wouldn't lie to him. "I can't, Ross." Her lower lip trembled. The scenario was all too reminiscent of what her husband had put her through—coming second. "I just can't."

"So why are you really upset, aside from the fact that Teddy and you both were disappointed?" Janey wanted to know after Eileen had confided her problems over the phone. "Surely you understand why Ross had to go." They both knew Eileen was equally committed to her work.

"I guess it was the attorney he took with him."

"Lenoir Collins," Janey surmised with a sigh.

"Yes."

"What upsets you the most? The fact that he's away or that he's away with a woman?"

As usual, Janey's observations were right on target. "That he's away with a woman," Eileen admitted reluctantly in a low tone. She wrapped her fingers around the phone cord. "But it's more than that." Eileen tried desperately to put her feeling into words. She swallowed hard. "She shares a common interest with Ross, something I don't. And he talks about her in such glowing terms."

"So don't you respect some of your male colleagues?"

"It's not the same," Eileen prickled defensively. "I don't go away on trips with them. And she's so young...just twenty-six." Probably beautiful, single. Available.

"Ross isn't Ted, Eileen. He won't play around simply because he's not at the usual 'home plate.'"

"I know that," she responded, her spine straightening defensively. She still felt inadequate, depressed.

"How much of this has to do with your birthday next week?" Janey guessed.

Eileen blushed. "I've been trying not to think about that!"

"Turning thirty can be traumatic. I know. That's one of the reasons we had our last child. Because I needed to feel my life wasn't over."

"You make it sound so melodramatic," Eileen mumbled.

"For a woman it is. Maybe men, too. They just show it in different ways. Men buy boats. Change careers. Get married, start families."

"They also get divorced. Trade in the 'old model' for a new sportier version. I'm scared, Janey—scared Ross isn't going to want me anymore once he remembers what it's like to be with someone who doesn't have a child's schedule or needs to cater to, someone who's free to concentrate only on him if the spirit moves her. Someone who could be with him whenever he wanted, someone who could spend the entire night."

"You're being ridiculous."

"I know that intellectually." Eileen sighed. "It's just my heart I'm having trouble convincing."

"You'll feel better when Ross is back in town, and that fateful birthday is over and you discover your days are still like the rest."

"I doubt it."

"Trust me. I've been there," her older sister soothed. "I know."

Janey was right, Eileen concluded after hanging up the phone. She was being ridiculous. If only she had been warmer to Ross when he'd called to say he couldn't make it, if only she'd been more understanding. The phone rang again just as she was getting into bed. A flicker of apprehension swept through her as she reached for the receiver. How she hoped it was Ross, checking in with her! For once, her dreams were answered.

"Hi," murmured Ross's deep sexy voice. "Just thought I'd check in with you to let you know where I was staying and see if everything's all right."

"I'm glad you called." Eileen pulled the receiver into bed with her. Taking a deep breath, she apologized, "I'm sorry I was angry when you had to leave." Even though he was hundreds of miles away, it was impossible to steady her erratic pulse or suppress the joy and relief bubbling up inside her.

He paused, as if groping for something appropriate to say. "I understand you were disappointed."

His generosity made her smile. "We both know that's no excuse. I reacted childishly." She'd been jealous. It was as simple and as complicated as that.

"Will you forgive me?" Her only defense was that she was madly, irrevocably in love with him.

"If you'll welcome me with open arms."

His gentle voice quelled the last of her fears. "l promise. How's the work going?"

"Better than I expected, actually. Lenoir brought her research along with her. We went over it on the plane. Looks like the plaintiff doesn't have a legal leg to stand on. We're hoping to wrap this up by tomorrow afternoon at the latest."

Again, jealousy surged up inside her. She fought it, refusing to succumb to the destructive emotion. Ross was just doing his job. She had to stop comparing him to Ted, Sr. Fists clenching tightly in her lap, she said maturely, "I'm glad your work is going so well."

"Do me a favor?" Ross said. "Pick me up at the airport? I don't want to be apart one second longer than necessary."

Recalling how he had held her the last time they were together, her body ached for his touch. "What time does your flight get in to the airport?"

"Late tomorrow evening, around ten."

She leaned back against the pillows, relaxing. Her voice was a husky whisper. "I'll be there," she promised. "And I'll be counting the minutes until then."

"Eileen? I really miss you." There was love deep in his voice.

"I miss you, too."

8

EILEEN WAS AT THE AIRPORT as scheduled. Heart pounding, she watched Ross stride out of the gate. A gorgeous young redhead, who she assumed was Lenoir Collins, was at his side smiling and talking the whole way. Eileen's heart sank as all her old fears and uncertainties were drafted back into action. Glancing up, Ross smiled dazzlingly when he saw her. Heedless of the others around him, he pulled her into his arms, his brief hard caress a wellspring of love and possession. "God, I missed you," he whispered, his breath hot against her ear.

She basked in the knowledge of his affection, and instantly relaxed. "I missed you, too."

Remembering himself at last, Ross belatedly made introductions. "Eileen, this is Lenoir Collins, a new attorney for my firm. Lenoir, I want you to meet a very special person in my life, Eileen Garrett."

"At long last, we meet!" Lenoir exclaimed delightedly, cradling her briefcase and flight bag in her arms. "You're really going to have to do something about this man of yours." Lenoir laughed pleasantly, facing them. Ross and Eileen stood together, his arm snugly wrapped about her shoulders. Lenoir shook her head ruefully, obviously quite unattached emotionally to her boss. "I have never in my entire life known a man to go on and on about the lady in his life. He never stopped talking about you. Teddy, either."

Ross looked at Eileen. "Speaking of Teddy, where is he?"

"I took him up to visit my folks this morning as scheduled."

Regret briefly lowered the corners of his mouth. "I'm sorry I missed him," Ross said softly. His luminous gaze said he would make up his absence to them both. *He really does love me,* she thought, rejoicing in the thought.

Gesturing freely, Ross continued, "I realized as soon as I got on the plane I didn't have any pictures of either you or Teddy in my wallet. We're going to have to remedy that right away."

Lenoir groaned and pressed a limp hand across her brow. "No doubt he would have been showing them to the flight attendants, too, had he possessed them."

"Hey, now." Ross finally took exception, his arm still anchored firmly around Eileen. "All I said was—"

"That you were in love with the most beautiful, wonderful woman on earth." Shaking her head in perplexity, Lenoir barely stifled a yawn. "And you had to get back to be with her."

"I was trying to make certain they got the plane off the ground on time." To Eileen's astonishment, Ross seemed not the least bit sheepish about proclaiming his devotion to her. Happiness flooded her.

More, it was suddenly clear to Eileen that Ross and his colleague were light-years apart, not just in age, but in outlook. "Marry him. Do us all a favor." Lenoir spied a young man coming toward her. "There's the love of *my* life." She waved, her face lighting up as she faced her beau. "Nice to meet you, Eileen. Ross, have a nice vacation. I'll see you when you get back. I've got to go."

As soon as Lenoir departed, Ross steered Eileen toward the exit. "I'm glad to be back."

"I'm glad to have you back." She held his arm tightly.

"Can you forgive me for spoiling the weekend?"

"Can you forgive me for being jealous?"

His eyebrows flickered a little. "Of my work?"

"Of Lenoir." Her face flamed as she wondered just how much to confess. But he had to know. She couldn't let him think, like his ex-wife, that she would ever try to undermine his devotion to his career. "I know it's silly, but—" She glanced at the toe of her sling-back pump. She had dressed up especially for him, in a lavender silk skirt and matching free-flowing skirt.

"You're serious, aren't you?" He stared down at her in awe.

"I know how ridiculous I was being. I'm just so scared of losing you." Her heart pounded with anxiety as she sought to make him understand.

"Because of Ted?" His curt voice lashed at her. Clearly, he resented the comparison to her husband.

That had been the least of it. She shook her head. "Because of you, Ross." Hands linked, they moved through the automatic doors and out into the starry summer night. A warm breeze caressed her skin and lifted the hem of her dress in a slow, sensuous swirl around her legs. Ross noticed, his eyes lingering, caressing. With difficulty she continued to explain, wanting him to understand now, before they were alone in bed, so that nothing negative would intrude on their reunion together. "Even when I was married to Ted, and knew—guessed—that he was being unfaithful, it didn't cut at me the way this out-of-town trip of yours did." She halted unexpectedly, pivoting to face him. Her head tilted back to better survey him. The soft yielding of her breasts brushed the hardness of his chest. "I'm in love with you, Ross. More than I'd ever thought it possible to love someone." Her heart was hammering foolishly in her chest. His closeness was so male, so bracing as to be nearly overwhelming. Her voice was a tremulous, yearning whisper. "It's going to take some time before I learn how to handle it." And the other women who would inevitably be working with and around him.

"Well, time we've got, Eileen." He put down his briefcase and the carry-on garment bag he'd slung over his shoulder and took her face between his large hands and cupped it gently. "All the time in the world...."

Together, they drove back to her home and made tender love through the night. She was the happiest she had ever been. But as always, morning came far too soon. And with it responsibilities Ross had been forced to put aside while he was out of town. "I'm going to have to go into the office this morning and go through my mail, clear up everything on my desk and assign the active cases I've got pending before we'll be free to leave for Bermuda as scheduled tomorrow morning. Think you can do without me for the rest of the day?" He paused, tucking his shirt into the waistband of his pants. He'd showered and changed into clean clothes from his overnight bag.

"Sure." She didn't want to, but she would. "As it happens, I've got a lot to do, too." The hours she had spent taking Teddy to her parents' farm had not left her much time to clean the house, and though she doubted Ross had noticed the clutter the evening before, her place did need a thorough cleaning.

Eileen was sitting cross-legged on the floor, wrestling with a recalcitrant vacuum cleaner when the doorbell rang a scant two and a half hours later. She opened the door to find Ross towering over her, arms crossed over his chest. Her hand lifted to the disarray of her hair, pulled back into a careless ponytail on the back of her head. She hadn't even had a chance to curl it after her shower. Yet he was looking at her as if she were Cinderella on the night of the ball. His glance raked her up and down approvingly, as he noted the faded cutoffs and apricot tank top. "I thought you were going in to the office," she asked, touching her hair self-consciously. She hated the thought of his seeing her when she was at such a disadvantage!

"I did. Couldn't concentrate, so I took care of what was absolutely essential and then said to heck with it, went home briefly, and came back." He lounged against the frame, his hands folded across his chest. He had changed into khaki sport shorts and a coordinating short-sleeved polo. How unglamorous to be caught cleaning and vacuuming. "Are you going to keep me out here all day or may I come in?"

Embarrassment sent a riot of color into her cheeks. "Uh, actually, Ross, I'm cleaning the house." Pine-scented ammonia cleaner filled the air, and there was polish and rags everywhere.

With a careless smile, he stalked past her and closed the door. "I don't mind a mess. I thought, since we were forced to cancel our bon-voyage party the other night, the two of us might drive up and see Teddy before we left for Bermuda. Your parents' farm isn't that far from here, is it?"

"It's an hour's drive at most." Did she want him to meet her folks, and they him? The answer was yes to both. Ross glanced at the vacuum cleaner sprawled across the floor. "What seems to be the problem with your appliance?"

How had she managed without him, ever? He was such an essential part of her life now. Absently, she answered his question. "It needs a new cord. I bought the kit and I'm trying to replace it myself." Actually, she'd been trying for the last half hour to take the darn machine apart, but hadn't gotten very far. Electrical cords were not her specialty.

Ross nodded, then volunteered, "Get me a pair of pliers and a pair of wire cutters if you have them. If not, any sharp paring knife will do. I'll fix it for you."

He started toward the machine. She followed, grateful to have him there. "If you don't mind, I'd like to watch. I want to know how to do it myself if the problem should happen again."

He shrugged genially, but sent her a quizzical glance. "Okay."

Hands on her hips, her mouth twisting ruefully, she confronted him. "You think I'm being ridiculous, that I should just let you do it and be done with it, don't you?"

"It would be simpler," he said with a significant lifting of his brows.

"Maybe now," she agreed, "but not in the long run. Look," she said raking a hand through her hair, wanting him not only to understand the reasons for, but approve of, her ruthlessly independent streak. "When I was married, my husband encouraged me to depend upon him for everything. He said he would take care of me. I believed him. I quit school because he wanted me to be able to travel with him when he played ball in different cities. I learned nothing about our finances. I couldn't even balance the checking account with any assurance of success. Hence when he died, I was penniless and pregnant. And though I could have run back home to my parents, I chose to go it alone. For the first time in my life, I was responsible for myself. The first years were hard on me, I don't deny it. But I have learned to cope on my own. I don't want to start leaning on you, not the way I leaned on Ted."

"Part of me wants to tell you you could lean on me for anything. The other half is glad you're independent."

"Then you do understand?"

"Hell, yes. The same was true for me when I broke up with my ex-wife. There was a lot about laundry and dishwashers I had to conquer. Once you've learned what it is to be on your own, independent and self-sufficient, there is no going back."

Was he trying to tell her in some unsubtle way he was against ever remarrying? She wondered. "I'll get the wire cutters." She choked out the words, turning miserably away. Maybe she had misunderstood. But her heart said differently. Once burned, twice wary. That was how he felt. She understood, because not too long ago she had felt that way herself. Now, loving Ross, for her everything had changed. She had realized while he was away that she wanted a permanent commitment from him. She wanted him to be a stable everyday part of her life, to be able to love her freely every night. She wanted him to have the legal right to live with them and be a real father to Teddy. She wanted to be married. But that obviously wasn't going to happen, at least not for a while, so in the meantime she would just have to be content with what they had. While she went to get the requested tools, he sat cross-legged on the floor and began effortlessly removing the cord from the engine. She patiently watched and assisted. Together, they finished the rudimentary household chores in record time, Eileen cleaning the smudges and dirt off her windows, Ross vacuuming the living room and stairs. The newly functioning machine switched off with a whine. Arms hooked around his knees, he was surveying her intently. She flushed. "I like watching you," he said softly. He moved over to touch up a cloudy spot on the glass next to the ceiling. When he'd finished, he let the blind snap down and in one swift motion drew her into his arms.

"What I feel for you scares me," she confided.

"It scares me, too. I couldn't think of anything but you and Teddy while I was in Chicago." He lowered his mouth to hers and indulged in a lengthy kiss. The rest of her doubts fell prey to his sensual persuasion as his hands swept under her top to undo the snap on her shorts. He cupped her buttocks with his palms, pressing her intimately against him. "God, you look beautiful," he breathed.

"I'm a mess."

"Not to me. You ought to see yourself, hair loose, cheeks flushed, those short cutoffs revealing every inch of suntanned thigh. I wanted to devour you the instant I saw you."

She grinned. "Why didn't you?"

He shrugged roguishly. "It probably had something to do with that warning glint in your eyes. The I-am-not-ready-to-see-you-I-look-a-mess look." Placing an arm beneath her knees, he swept her up off her feet and carried her up the stairs. He didn't stop until they reached her bed. The blinds of the second-floor window slanted slightly in. She glanced toward them. He said, "Leave them open. I want to see you in the sunlight." His thumb moved to rest on her lips, silencing her tenderly. "I want you to see me."

His reasoning was hard to resist. They undressed in a slow, sensual series of movements, stopping at length to kiss and caress and learn each other's bodies and penchants once again. Naked, they swayed together languorously, her arms wreathed around his neck, his laced low around her hips. Her knees weakened, her pulse fluttered as he led her back toward the freshly changed sheets on her bed. "Tell me you need me," he whispered against the lobe of her ear.

"I need you." She arched against him, tantalized by the knowing certainty of his touch.

"And that I'm the only man in your life." His eyes darkened with the intensity of his passion.

Her need for him consumed her, making everything hazy and light and slightly ethereal. "You're the only man who's ever been in my life." He was the only man she had ever loved with all of a woman's heart.

Ross was hot and throbbing as he lay down beside her. Needing to dominate, to possess, he removed the pillows from under her head so she lay flat and completely vulnerable on the mattress beneath him. His hands moved down over her ribs, past the concavity of her stomach, to the golden-brown delta that proclaimed her a woman. She shuddered at his touch, a purr of pleasure emanating from low in the back of her throat. He anchored her ankles with his hands and, whispering her name, made a lazy trail up her thighs. He tasted, kissed, laved. His fingers covered her silken flesh, sliding into her, upward. "Ross—" Her hands caught in his hair, pulling him upward. They kissed languidly, mouths melded together, infusing each other with ever-increasing heat. She whimpered ecstatically against the hot pressure of his mouth and the seeking motion of his fingers as they tested the dewy moisture within.

And then he was on top of her, pushing her to the edge of the double bed. "I want you," he murmured roughly, rapaciously, the full length of his body luxuriously covering hers, "so much."

Her shoulders were even with the mattress edge, her hair falling in a burnished cloud to the floor. She felt desire as she had never imagined it possible, as part of her, part of him. Desire: inevitable and indomitable, something to be coveted, something to be feared, something to be attained. He touched her again, intimately, in a way that banished shame and invited only pleasure. And then he was one with her, moving inside her, slowly at first, with great restraint and then deeper, ever deeper, like fire to her flame. He moaned, a low guttural sound that caused shivers to slide over her skin. Her arms and legs wrapped around him. Setting the rhythm, delaying, he covered her mouth with another long hungry kiss that was as deep as it was ardent. She opened herself up to him, body and soul, welcoming his maleness, needing his strength. The world was bedazzled, burning, melting. Her breasts were exquisitely tender, pressed flat against his chest. Culmination was like free-falling off the edge of the earth, crescendo, decrescendo, ever softer, ever loving, ever sweet. She clung to him long afterward, the salty taste of her skin mingling with his. Marriage no longer seemed to matter. She had him, and that was all that counted.

TEDDY WAS DELIGHTED TO SEE ROSS when they arrived at her parents' farm later that afternoon. The five of them toured the acreage, viewing both the animals and the shoulder-high corn, before settling down to a home-style country barbecue supper, eaten at a leisurely pace out-of-doors. Finally, around seven-thirty, Eileen and Ross admitted they really had to go. Teddy, happy to remain with his grandparents,

who admittedly spoiled him rotten, was not the least
bit difficult about their departure. Her parents approved heartily of Ross, she could tell, and were
even more pleased that she had brought Ross home
to meet them. "Janey mentioned you'd been seeing
someone wonderful," her mother said, walking her
to the car. "You don't know how happy that makes
your father and me."

"As happy as it makes me?" She felt as if her face
had been gifted with a permanent smile.

"I doubt anyone could be that happy," her mother
said dryly.

"Ross, we're glad you could come up," her father
remarked genially as he and Ross shook hands. Eileen embraced her parents affectionately, then knelt
to give a last hug to her son. "Be good for grandma
and grandpa now while I'm away."

"I will," Teddy said. His small face turned up toward hers earnestly. "And mom...have a good
time." Smiling shyly, he looked at his coach. "You,
too, Ross."

"We will," Ross promised.

BECAUSE THEIR FLIGHT LEFT EARLY the next morning, Ross
spent the evening at her place. He was up early, putting his suitcases in the car. Eileen was still dressing
when he lithely mounted the stairs to her bedroom.
"All set?" He stood framed in the door.

"Almost." She put on the earrings he had given
her, then ran a quick brush through her hair and
followed it with a light spray. She'd selected a sum-
mery white dress with waist-length short-sleeved
jacket and sandals. He was dressed in pleated linen
trousers, striped sport shirt and tie. Eileen looked
down at the cosmetic case, checking to make sure
she hadn't forgotten anything.

His glance dropped to the three suitcases open on her bed. "Tell me you don't plan to take all of these," he groaned.

Facetiously, she repeated in a deadpan tone, "I don't plan to take all of them." Her glittering, exhilarated gaze said differently. "Of course I plan to take all of them!" This was to be her first real vacation out of the continental United States. She didn't plan to leave any of her favorite garments behind.

Without warning, his mouth twisted into a rueful grin. "Whatever makes you happy," he murmured.

"You make me happy." She glided forward to press a light kiss to his lips.

His arms laced around her waist invitingly. "Show me more," he coaxed in a silken drawl.

"When we arrive in paradise," she promised. Venturing a glance at her watch, she said, "And unless we want to miss our flight altogether, we had better be going."

They had breakfast en route to Atlanta, then switched to a British Airways jet. Settling back in their seats, sipping celebratory Mimosas—orange juice and champagne—they spied the dark blue-gray of the ocean through the fluffy white layers of cumulus dotting the sky below. Her hand entwined safely with Ross's strong palm, Eileen had never been happier. Her only cause for nervousness was the prospect of meeting his teenage son. For all their sakes, she wanted the boy to like her.

"Does your son, Steve, know I'm coming with you?" Eileen asked as casually as she could manage.

"Yes, I called him and told him a few days ago, right after we'd first decided to take the trip together. Why?" He faced her curiously.

Hesitation made her tense. "Will he resent my presence?" she asked carefully at last. "I know you don't see him very often. I wouldn't want to intrude or take away what should be a very happy private reunion between the two of you."

"You won't disrupt anything, Eileen. Steve knows how I feel about you, that you're very important to me. And unless he's changed greatly since I last saw him, which I doubt, you can count on him to behave well." His smiled widened in approval, successfully disarming her. "But for the record, I'm glad you're so caring."

She wondered if he wasn't being hopelessly optimistic under the circumstances, but said nothing more. Talk turned to more casual matters during the rest of the flight, and as the plane lowered in altitude for the final descent and the island became visible, her excitement rose. Bermuda was a scant twenty-one miles long, situated atop a subterranean mountain. As they descended, she could see pink-tinged sandy beaches surrounded by a glittering turquoise sea. Limestone houses with distinct pastel icing on the roofs sparkled in the sun. Cars were conspicuously absent from the roads, but there was an abundance of buses and motorbikes.

The island was hot and gloriously sunny when they deplaned. After collecting all their luggage and securing a blue-flagged taxi to the hotel, Ross checked them into a housekeeping cottage at the Cambridge Beaches in Sandys Parrish. It was a lovely secluded twenty-five-acre estate on Mangrove Bay. The whole resort was surrounded by water, with beaches on three sides. An outdoor terrace overlooked the bay.

An hour after lunch, Ross's son arrived. Eileen was understandably nervous as the three of them gathered on the hotel terrace for a cool drink. At fourteen, Steve was lanky and tall and—like his father—handsome and outgoing. He wore pleated khaki trousers and a Lacoste shirt. Steve was charming, with a dazzling smile. His hair was shot through with bronze and gold streaks and was cut in a preppy, ultrashort fashion. Her heart warmed at the affection displayed between the two of them as she watched them embrace. "Dad." Steve's voice was choked with emotion.

"I can't believe how you've grown." Ross's eyes were luminous, shimmering with affection. Turning, he made introductions. Steve greeted her graciously, but with a certain reserve. *He's wary of me,* she thought, clutching the gift she had brought for him in her hands. *And with good reason. I'm also important to his dad.* She was going to have to tread very carefully where the child's heart and security were concerned.

"I thought we'd rent mopeds and see some of the island this afternoon," Ross said eventually, after they'd all finished their iced tea. "That is, if you're amenable, Steve?" His son nodded affably, as did Eileen when Ross cast a questioning glance her way. Rental cars were not allowed on the island for fear of further congesting traffic.

While Ross went to see about renting the mopeds in the hotel lobby, Eileen gave Steve her gift. He glanced down at the Dungeons and Dragons module with keen interest.

"I know from talking to your dad you attend school in England," Eileen explained. "I had no idea what sort of games were played there, other than the usual chess and checkers, and maybe Monopoly or Parcheesi. I thought maybe you'd enjoy this for a change."

"Yes, I will. And it *is* something I don't have." He looked up at her, gratitude evident in his eyes. "Thanks."

"You're welcome."

They chatted on briefly about the weather and how wonderfully invigorating the sea breeze was. Finally, Steve cut through the civilities to ask curiously, softly, "Eileen, are you going to marry my dad?" He had fair skin that had been sunburned, and what seemed to be a perpetually peeling nose. His lashes were long and silky, equally as light as his hair.

"I don't know," she said honestly.

Steve seemed to want assurance that she wouldn't hurt or use Ross. Relief flowed through her. Those kind of anxieties she could quell. How awful, she thought, only to see your father at a few intervals during the year. Teddy might never have his father now, but at least he wasn't deprived of companionship due to a parental difference of opinion. How much harder that must be for a child to accept, she mused. Death was irrevocable. Divorce was not.

"We are very good friends," she said finally, for want of a better term. "But we haven't made any definite plans."

Steve nodded acceptingly, leaning back in his chair. "Dad says you have a little boy."

Eileen smiled. "Yes, I have a son. Teddy. He's nine." She wondered briefly if Teddy would be as lanky and physically awkward as Steve when he reached adolescence.

"Does dad spend time with him?" Steve rubbed his knuckles back and forth on the palm of his other hand. His eyes met hers directly, and she couldn't do anything but tell him the truth.

"Yes, they get along very well, as a matter of fact. Your father coaches him in his Little League team in Indianapolis."

Steve thought that over. Apparently, feeling it no

threat, he said finally, "If you did marry, would my dad adopt your son, since he doesn't have a father? Dad told me on the phone you were a widow," he added at her questioning look.

Eileen sighed raggedly. She was beginning to see that teenagers could be every bit as demanding as nine year olds, only in different ways. "I don't know."

"But you'd want him to."

"Yes. I suppose." Abruptly, Steve scowled. And for understandable reasons, considering all the day-to-day attention Teddy received from Ross, attention Steve must crave. For no matter how attentive a stepfather and mother was, Steve would always want the paternal link he remembered. He would always in his heart wish their initial family unit had stayed intact. And she couldn't blame him.

At that instant, Ross came back into the room. He looked from one to the other. The tension in the air was palpable. "What have the two of you been talking about?" Although his tone was genial, Ross assessed Eileen with unrelenting scrutiny. He obviously expected her to tell him if Steve had been giving her a hard time.

"Steve and I were just getting to know each other," Eileen said pleasantly. Later, she'd tell Ross what a fine son he had. "How did the arrangements go?"

Ross smiled, looking greatly relieved. "We're all set. We can pick up the mopeds right now."

The slight awkwardness melted away miraculously as, laughing and talking with increasing animation, the three of them explored the narrow winding Bermuda roads. They enjoyed the breathtaking views of the sea and the shore and the sight of colorful subtropical flowers and plants that graced every byway. Oleander and hibiscus hedges dominated the scenery, and the air was fresh and fragrant, the sky overhead marvelously sunny and blue. At Ross's suggestion, they took the ferry across the Great Sound to Somerset Bridge and explored the village shops. Then, at Steve's urging, they took a glass-bottomed-boat trip from Mangrove Bay over the coral reefs. After a brief swim, the trio returned for dinner at a local inn, then put Steve in a taxi back to his mother and stepfather's elegant home off Warwick Road.

"Well, what do you think?" an exhausted Eileen asked, sinking down onto a chair and kicking off her sandals the moment they entered their room. "Was the day a success?"

"Steve adores you!" Ross beamed.

Eileen grinned, warming at the thought of the afternoon they had spent together. "It was an enjoyable day." She gave Ross a tentative, teasing glance. "I think Steve and I are beginning to get along."

"I'm almost jealous of the attention he gives you." Ross made a show of miming an exaggerated sulk.

"You're teasing." She let him draw her to her feet and take her tenderly into his arms. His arms encircled her, one hand in the small of her back, until he felt her conform to his length with just the right amount of yielding surrender.

"Yes. About being jealous. Not about this." Satisfied with the complete harmony of their bodies, his hand moved to the first button on her dress as his mouth covered hers, then ever so gently teased her lips apart, so he might have better, more passionate access to the honeyed caverns of her mouth. "Or this...." His other hand slid across her thigh, to tug and then lift the hem of her full dirndl skirt. "Or this...."

It was a very long, romantic night, with Ross proving with actions and words how very special she was to him, and she returning the affection tenfold, until at last, exhausted and sated, they slept, wrapped in each other's arms.

The days that followed were equally blissful. The three of them visited the Maritime Museum and Royal Keepyard, the *Deliverance*, a replica of one of the first ships built on the island in 1609, historic Fort Hamilton, and the Crystal Cave. Several evenings Steve dined with them. Several were spent alone, including their next-to-last evening on the island.

As was the custom in Bermuda, they dressed formally for their evening out together. In lieu of renting a taxi to take them to their destination, however, Ross surprised her with a horse-drawn-carriage ride to the prestigious Waterlot Inn restaurant. They dined by candlelight on the outdoor terrace, feasting on *l'entrecôte au poivre Toulouse-Lautrec*—pepper steak flamed at the table. For dessert they enjoyed *la coupe Fosco*—homemade raspberry and orange sherbet with fresh strawberries and sherry melba sauce. Another horse-drawn carriage took them back to their hotel. Ross ordered a bottle of champagne from room service, and when it arrived they shucked off their shoes and ventured down to the deserted starlit private beach.

When both champagne and conversation were exhausted, Ross dug into the pocket of his elegant black jacket. "I wanted to save this for an appropriate moment.'

She sent him a quizzical glance as she accepted the

small blue velvet jewelry box. "Open it," he commanded gently.

With trembling fingers, she complied. "Oh, Ross..." she said, fingering the elegant strand of leaf and diamond necklace.

"Happy birthday," he said softly.

"Who told you?" she demanded. Incredulous as it seemed, she'd forgotten.

"Janey. She said you'd been depressed—"

"I'm always depressed on my birthday." She turned toward him imploringly, handing over the delicate strand. "Will you do the honors?"

"Gladly." He fastened the chain, then traced the design where it lay against the lightly tanned skin of her throat. "I always felt you should have everything. In reality, you seem to have had so little," he murmured.

Maybe monetarily—certainly, she was no jet-setter. But those kinds of things had never mattered to her. "I have everything I ever need or want in you," she murmured, lacing her hands around his neck. Pulling his head down to hers, she thanked him in a very special private way.

When the slow, sweet kiss had ended he drew back. "Then maybe, just maybe, it's also time for this," he said softly. With a hint of humor gleaming enigmatically in his eyes, he handed her a tiny blue velvet jewelry box. *More earrings,* she wondered. But he'd already given her a pair. She flicked open the lid. Inside was the most beautiful diamond solitaire she'd ever seen in her life.

"Ross—" Shock stole the breath from her lungs, making her voice little more than a stunned whisper.

He watched her with an intensity that only heightened her joy.

"You didn't think I would ask you to accompany me here unless I was serious, did you?" He slipped the ring from the box and slid it over her finger. It was, as she had suspected it would be, a perfect fit. "I love you," he said huskily. "I want you to marry me. I'll make you happy. I'll be a good father to Teddy, I promise."

The possibility of their union was everything she had ever wanted and so much more. "Yes, oh yes," she whispered tremulously, tears of joy misting her eyes, clinging to her lashes. He drew her to him, his arms wrapped tightly around her, his erratic heartbeat pressed against her own. His lips found hers, gently traversing the parted curves, kissing her so thoroughly she could not breathe. She returned the endearment with a passionate intensity that made them both tremble with yearning. Arm in arm, stopping frequently along the way to wonderingly kiss and caress each other, they returned to their room. Once inside, Ross reached over to draw the drapes. With his arms wrapped around her, his kiss was shimmering, rippling fire as he drew her down softly to the bed.

The touch of his hands upon her was almost unbearable in their exquisite tenderness as he undressed her, and then she, him. She tasted and touched every texture of his skin. Conscious of where his naked skin rubbed against hers, she felt as if she would never be able to explore him intimately, deeply enough. His slow, drugging kisses sent a sweet song of passion humming through her veins. Her skin felt soft and supple wherever he touched, until at last she was gathered against his strong pulsing body, his hands skimming down either side of her back to her thighs. His knees wedged entry between her own. Wordlessly, he brought her hand to him, then watched, eyes shuttered with the intensity of all he was feeling, as she slowly guided his entrance to first her body, and then, inevitably, her heart. A moan of ecstasy slipped through her lips and then she shattered into a million spinning pieces as they soared together to the ardent heights of their souls.

When at last the sensual storm had ended, and she was gathered, replete and breathless against him, Eileen stirred, murmuring into his shoulder, "I love you, Ross. I love you."

"I know." His arms tightened around her possessively, and there was both fierce satisfaction and wonderment in his voice. "I know...."

9

ON ROSS AND EILEEN'S LAST MORNING in Bermuda, they took Steve horseback riding and then rented a boat and motored contentedly around the island one last time. They returned to the hotel terrace overlooking the bay, looking suntanned and happy. While Ross went back to the bungalow to shower and change clothes, Eileen kept Steve company as he sipped an iced fruit drink and hungrily munched on a plate of hot cheese and crabmeat hors d'oeuvres. "I'm sorry I was so suspicious of your motives for coming here that first day," Steve confessed, embarrassment coloring his cheeks and the tips of his ears.

Eileen smiled sympathetically. In the short time they'd spent together, she'd grown to love Ross's son, feeling nearly as close to him as she did to either Teddy or her nephew, Brian. "That's okay. I know how you must feel. Usually the summer weeks are just between the two of you men, aren't they?"

"Yeah." Steve looked sheepishly down at his plate. "But I want you to know that I had an even better time with you along. Dad was more relaxed than he usually is—more fun to be with this time." He grinned wickedly, with a glint of humor in his eyes very much like his father's. "You must make him feel younger."

"That goes double," she mused aloud whimsically. No longer did turning thirty and beginning a new decade of her life seem the least bit depressing. Instead, it was as if a whole new aspect of her life had opened up. Ross made her feel fresh, new, as if she existed only for him.

Steve swallowed a few more snacks, stretched his legs restlessly out before him. *He's almost grown*, Eileen thought, with a pang of parental empathy for Ross. How quickly the years could pass. And he had missed so much time with his only son.

"You're very close to your father, aren't you?"

Steve nodded. "When my folks first got divorced, I was afraid I'd never see my dad again, that it wouldn't be the same. But even after all these years of me living in Europe and Bermuda, and him in the States, I still feel like a part of him. Like on Tuesday, when I was complaining about the amount of work I had to do at prep school, he started lecturing me about how important it was to put forth my best effort. Since he only sees me a couple of weeks a year, he doesn't have to act like that. He could just try and have a good time with me. But he doesn't. He really cares." As if embarrassed by how much he'd revealed, Steve ducked his head, looking out at the wharf. "That's why I was a little suspicious when I saw you that first day. He'd never brought anyone here with him before. I was afraid if the two of you did get married and he adopted your son that he might not want to see me anymore."

"Oh, Steve, don't you know how much you mean to your dad? He loves you. You're his first son, his only child. Even if he adopted Teddy or eventually had more children, nothing would alter the way he feels about you. You'll always be important to him."

His eyes sparkled, reminding her of Ross's charm. "Anyway, I just wanted you to know I'm glad you're getting married."

"Thanks." She smiled shyly. "It means a lot to me, knowing you approve."

Ross appeared at the edge of the terrace. Pulling up a chair, he sat down beside her. "What's the powwow about?" he asked curiously.

Eileen's mouth curved upward. "We were discussing your virtues again."

"Oh?" His brows shot up as a pleased smile lit his face. "Do continue."

She shook her head and kissed the top of his head, then bent and did the same to Steve. "If it's an affidavit of love you need, counselor, you're going to have to get it from your son." She knew their last goodbyes should be spent alone, man to man, with no friend or fiancée, no matter how close, around to intrude. "I'll see you later," she said softly to Ross. "Steve, I'm glad we met."

He smiled dazzlingly in return. "I'm glad we met, too."

"I HATE TO SEE OUR VACATION come to an end," Ross remarked later, placing an arm around her waist. They were strolling hand in hand down the beach, both barefoot, she carrying her sandals and stockings, he his socks and shoes. "I'm going to miss sleeping with you, waking to find you by my side," he confessed. "The only time we've been apart was when I took Steve scuba diving earlier in the week." She'd gone into Hamilton and browsed through the many gift shops on Front Street.

"I'll miss you, too," she agreed. As his hands came up to briefly cup her face, she leaned against him, hot, wild, yearning. Would it go on like this forever, she wondered wistfully. Heaven knew she wanted it to with all her heart and soul, would do anything to keep it just so. Moonlight spilled down over the water, shimmering against the darker surface of the sea. The surf pounded in the distance. The soft coral sand was warm and wet beneath their feet, the water only slightly cooler than it had been that afternoon. She knew she would cherish forever the memory of their nights together, of happy days spent getting to know his son and of romantic dinners alone and feverish lovemaking that had often continued to nearly dawn. No man had ever demanded as much from her in bed, no one had ever bestowed upon her such bedazzling ardor. She had a constant heart-in-her-throat feeling whenever she was around him. "I want to be alone with you, in bed," he said huskily.

"Yes." Just one word, but it spoke volumes about the way she felt. In response, his eyes darkened with pleasure, his lips briefly caressed hers, then withdrew. Desire shimmered through her, as tangible and restless as the sea.

In romantic reverie, arms entwined about each other's waists, thighs brushing with every step, they crossed the pink-tinged beach once more and made their way slowly toward the cottage. Ross followed her into the sitting room, his hands laced around her waist, then wordlessly swung her around to face him. Deliberately, he pulled her against him, then bent slightly to bring his mouth into delicate contact with hers. She traced the sensual line of his mouth with her tongue and then shivered in response as he did the same to hers. Her arms wound around his neck as he deepened the kiss with a passionately rough demand that sent streamers of fire racing through her limbs. She clung to him, needing, wanting, yearning to give so much. Breathless moments later, he withdrew to promise huskily, "I'll call room service and have them send us some champagne."

She wanted to prolong their last evening together,

too, draw out each second until they practically screamed with their mutual hunger. Her eyes held his. "I'd like that."

He leaned forward, the muscles of his chest smooth and hard beneath his shirt. As her fingertips caressed and enjoyed the strength he held in check his slow smile was a tremulous slash against the tan of his face. He exhaled unevenly. "Have I thanked you yet for making this vacation the best week of my life?" As he murmured, his lips tenderly touched the curve of her cheek.

Mutely, she shook her head then, pulling his head down to hers, again found his mouth. They kissed lingeringly, wonderingly, until a knock at the door heralded room service's arrival. While he went to accept the champagne, she slipped into the bedroom, shedding her evening dress in favor of a negligee she'd been waiting all week to wear. He strode back in the door, carrying the ice bucket and long-stemmed glasses. He stopped when he saw her, pirouetting around to face him from her place at the mirror, his expression as pleased and surprised as she had hoped it would be.

"Do you like it?" She wore a white antique lace nightshift, cut low across the breasts. It was translucent and trimmed in blue ribbon. The hue of her aureoles was visible beneath the thin lacy cloth.

"That's the understatement of the year! You look... magnificent... desirable... ethereal," he said huskily. His eyes bored into hers, his intent unmistakable.

A warm flush of pleasure crept across her face. The corners of her mouth lifted, radiating the happiness within, which bubbled over whenever he was near. He set the champagne aside and crossed to her side, his hands spanned her waist through the translucent fabric.

Leaning into his seductive warmth, she admitted, "I picked it up in one of those exclusive shops on my solo shopping expedition in Hamilton." She'd wanted to make this night memorable. She'd wanted to be for him what no other woman could be.

His fingertips caressed what his eyes had admired, and a shiver went through her. She stopped his wandering hand, cautioning, "I have one more surprise, something I think you'll like." Taking him by the hand, she led him into the bathroom, toward the large marble tub, slowly filling with frothy white bubbles and hot water.

The corners of his mouth lifted in a devilish grin as he reached for the buttons on his shirt. "Good idea." She stopped his motion, her hand clasping his wrist.

"No," she corrected softly, "this is my treat." He had given her so much. Now it was her turn to please him. While the tub filled, she undressed him tenderly. He watched, mesmerized, overcome with delight. Her desire to please him touched him, made him vulnerable in a way mere words never could have.

"You're enchanting," he murmured, his eyes never leaving her.

"So are you."

He was ready for her as she drew down the elastic of his briefs and shucked them from his legs. As Ross reached for her, however, she drew back and directed him instead into the tub. Donning a soapy bath mitt she scrubbed his back, shoulders, chest, before sliding down to caress his thighs and ankles. Water splashed her gown, molding the material to her heated skin. Ross touched her breast, his hand cupping the lacy gauze, coaxing the confining material back and forth across her flesh until the nipple sprang impudently to life. "Come in here with me," he coaxed.

She wanted him more than life itself, but stronger than that was her need to make this a night to remember. And that would only be done by savoring every moment until the very last. "The champagne," she protested.

Eluding his touch, she fled the room, her hips swaying provocatively beneath the sheer gown. She heard his gasp, followed immediately by the teasing threat, "Thirty more seconds, Eileen, or I'm coming out." If he did that, the tryst would be run by his rules.

Breathless and giggling, she returned to the doorway, a glass of brimming champagne in each hand. "You win. I'm coming in," she purred when he moved as if to get out. Handing him the glass, she sipped from hers. Then, she lifted the floor-length hem of her gown to her knees, lifted one ankle and submerged it nearly to the knee in the depths of the warm water. He gazed at her hungrily then watched as slowly she peeled off the gown and joined him.

He swallowed hard. "I feel as if I'm about nineteen, and believe me I thought that would never happen again!"

She knelt between his thighs, facing him. They toasted the evening, they toasted each other. They celebrated their love. They kissed long and sweetly until her toes curled and her back arched in abandonment. Ross set both glasses aside and turning her, positioned her so she was sitting between his thighs, her back against his chest. She leaned her head back against his shoulder as he stroked her neck lightly with the tips of his fingers, and tilted her head back underneath his to the side, allowing him better access to her mouth. They kissed again. She was totally at his mercy, surrounded with love. One of his hands was fondling her breast, the other sweeping across the expanse of her abdomen to the silky juncture of her thighs. He stroked, probed within, seeking every secret place, and then used the bath mitt until she groaned, writhing and twisting against him. His thighs crushed inward as he held her in an indomitable embrace.

"Do you want me?" he asked, teasing her as she had teased him with her slow striptease.

"Yes!" So much so that she was on fire, every nerve ending in riotous flames.

"Now?" He traced the rim of her ear with his tongue and then lifted her hair, kissing the sensitive area at the base of her neck with a chasteness she found even more arousing.

"Yes, I want you here." Arms guiding her, assisting, he turned her toward him, so they were once again face to face. She straddled his thighs, feeling him slide up and into her. Their bodies fit—as hot and liquid as the steaming fragrant water around them. She wove her fingers through his hair, her nipples pressed against his chest. And they kissed and kissed, their tongue stroking in the same compelling rhythm as their love-heated flesh.

"I love holding you like this," he said. "I never want to stop."

Ross traced slow circles around her nipples, following the path with the gentle glide of his tongue until the pink-tipped circles were saucily erect, pulsing with the need for further stimulation. Then he closed his lips around her passion-heavy flesh, tugging sweetly.

"I want you," she gasped between gentle flicks of his tongue on her breasts. An ache rose like a river of passion inside her body.

"No, not yet." He forced her to slow down, hold back, firmly taking control.

"Ross—" His mouth fused with hers, his tongue

teasing along the inside of her lips. He knew all the moves to make her vulnerable and used every one.

"Let me lead." He scattered tantalizing kisses on the soft underside of her throat, continuing languidly until she surrendered, weak and passive against him, until she was throbbing as insistently and rhythmically as was he. "Now?" he asked hoarsely, when she'd given herself over to his control.

"Now," she begged. They scaled the heights of ecstasy together, her response more wild and wanton than it had ever been, his more demanding, more giving, more coaxing. Need gripped them both, then mounted to liquid fire and melting surrender. Slowly, still entwined, they drifted back down to reality.

Much later, he wrapped her in a towel and they moved to the bed, their bodies still tingling. Talking, laughing and teasing, they finished the rest of the champagne, then woke again to make love during the night and yet again before dawn.

"Don't ever leave me," he cried hoarsely. "I couldn't bear it."

"I won't." She cuddled closer to his chest, loving him, needing to hear the steady thrum of his heartbeat, feel the strength in the masculine arms around her.

"I love you," he whispered, holding her closer yet.

Happiness flowed through Eileen. "I love you, too." Tomorrow the vacation would end with the journey back to the States, but the loving would go on and on. Ross was in her life to stay.

"GOSH, I MISSED YOU GUYS." Teddy laced his arms about both their waists, hugging them as if he'd never get enough affection from them. Though Eileen and Ross had picked him up at her parents' farm hours earlier, he was still clinging to them both as if his life depended upon it.

Ross rubbed his jaw thoughtfully, feigning perplexity. "I guess this means then you're too happy to eat now, hmm?"

"No way!" Teddy shouted. "What *are* we going to have for dinner, mom?" he asked, releasing his hold on her.

Eileen groaned. So things were back to normal already, were they? "Your favorite question, asked at least fifty times every day," she teased.

"How about McDonald's?" Ross queried, guessing correctly she was too tired from their trip home the previous day to cook.

"Sounds great!" Teddy enthused. "Mom, what do you think?" He turned to her imploringly, hands clasped together in a mutely praying fashion.

"It sounds fine." Affectionately, she tousled his mass of blond hair. Later, after they'd eaten, she and Ross would tell him their news.

"So what did you do while we were gone?" Ross queried Teddy as they ate French fries and hamburgers.

"Oh, everything! Fed the horses and cows and watched grandma's chickens hatch in the incubator. Boy, mom, that was neat! You should have seen it!"

"I have—several times," she reminded.

"Oh, yeah." Teddy shrugged. "Well then, next time maybe we should take Ross."

She exchanged an endearing glance with her lover. "Maybe we will."

"So what did you do in Bermuda?" Teddy countered, dipping his French fries liberally in catsup. Ross told Teddy about the sailing and scuba diving and ferry rides around the island. "Sounds like fun," her son offered somewhat reluctantly when

Ross had finished. Teddy looked momentarily jealous, as if for the first time wishing he'd been included on the excursion.

Ross and Eileen exchanged a glance. At her nod, Ross said gently, "Your mother and I were thinking of taking you there, too, for a brief visit in August, before school. We'd like you to meet my son, Steve."

"He's very nice, Teddy. I think you'll like him," Eileen added. "And he knows a lot about baseball, too, though I think he could use some help with Dungeons and Dragons. I wasn't very good at explaining how the game is played."

"That's because you never play it," Teddy replied.

"Well, maybe you could teach him," Ross suggested.

Teddy nodded agreeably. "Maybe I will."

When dinner had ended, they drove out to the park. As they gathered the bats, balls, gloves and caps out of Ross's car for an impromptu catch-up batting session, Eileen said, sensing the time and the mood were both right, "That's not the only surprise we have for you, Teddy."

"Oh yeah, what?" He turned toward her curiously, shoving the brim of his cap away from his brow. "You already gave me a bunch of presents, so that can't be it."

This was a present, too, of sorts. The best and most precious kind. Eileen felt a lump welling up in her throat. Determinedly, moisture pricking her eyes, she plowed on, "How would you feel about Ross becoming your dad?"

For a second Teddy looked stunned, as if briefly he thought she were trying to give him away. "As in married," Ross explained dryly. "Me and your mom. Together. Wedding bells. Rice. Lots of crying and hugging and kissing. A two-car garage."

"Oh, great!" Teddy's shout of joy could have been heard clear across town as he gave up his ball and his bat and hurtled himself into both their arms once again. "Great! Great! Great!"

Without a doubt, Eileen thought, tears of happiness streaming down her face, *this is one of the best moments of my life.* When Ross squeezed her hand affectionately, she knew he thought so, too.

Teddy paused long enough to ask, "When is all this going to happen? I mean, is it soon?" Clearly, it couldn't be fast enough for him.

"We thought maybe the end of August," Ross said. "Before summer ends and school starts, though we haven't set an exact date yet." They'd wanted to go back to work first, check their schedules, give Teddy time to adjust. "Is that all right with you?"

"All right? It's terrific," Teddy enthused. "I feel like my best wish just came true."

Eileen couldn't have agreed more.

10

EILEEN EXPECTED TO BE CONFRONTED with a mountain of work to catch up on when she returned to her job in Indianapolis the following Monday morning. Instead, the bank manager asked to see her. He wasted no time with amenities, but got straight to the point. "Frankly, Eileen, you're one of the best loan officers we have in this company. In particular we admire the competent, professional way you have protected the rights and privacy of our clients. We're also impressed with how well you've handled the recurring problems with our local credit bureau. Now we'd like to put your talents to better use. Specifically, there's an opening for an assistant bank manager at our Gary, Indiana branch, in the northern part of the state. We'd like you to take it."

Eileen was stunned. She sat gripping the arms of her chair, her thoughts in turmoil. She had worked hard progressing to her present position, and if she hadn't been engaged to Ross she would have accepted the promotion in a minute. Finding her voice, she said finally, "Thank you. I don't know what to say. Did you know that I've just gotten engaged to be married?"

"I suspected it was coming, Eileen. But couldn't the wedding be put off temporarily or delayed? Or better yet, couldn't you go ahead and get married and then take turns commuting alternate weekends or whatever? Gary is only one hundred and fifty miles away." He knew full well she was used to managing on her own.

The bank manager continued affably, "Look, I know what we're asking would mean a sacrifice on your part, but when you consider the benefits over the long run, I do feel they're worth it. If this works out, you could be on the Board of Directors here one day. You could be named a vice-president of our firm. It would mean a great deal of financial security for your son and yourself as well as your new husband, though I understand Ross Mitchell isn't in need of any financial assistance."

That was part of the problem, Eileen thought mournfully. If Ross were less secure financially, his reaction would be quite different, and he might move with her. Other husbands sometimes did. But Ross? One of the most successful attorneys in the state?

"We'd want you to stay there and train for about a year," the bank manager continued. "Then if it worked out, we would transfer you back here, where you would assume a similar responsibility. It's quite an honor, Eileen. One I counsel you not to discard lightly."

"I'm aware of that and I'm very... pleased to have been selected for the job. But it isn't anything I can rush into, either." The thought of living without Ross, even for a while, took all the joy out of this offer.

"Naturally, we'd pay all your moving and living expenses. You could rent a place in Gary and keep your home here. We'd put you on an expense account and pay the mortgage until you returned. We're aware, of course, that you'd have to make arrangements for your son's care. We'd help you there in any way that we could. Since it's summer, you'd have no trouble enrolling your son in school before the start of the new year. He'd also have time to get acquainted with some of the local children before the fall term starts. If you accept the position, we'd like you to start August first."

"When do you need an answer?" Eileen asked.

"By the end of the week."

EILEEN MET ROSS FOR LUNCH to discuss the job opportunity with him. He accepted the news with obvious distress. "What will happen if you don't take the job?"

"I'll never be more than a senior loan officer at the bank. Although they would never come right out and say so, they look upon this as a test of my devotion to the company and my job."

The lines of concentration deepened around his eyes, across his forehead above his brows. "Would that bother you, if you stayed here, and then didn't move up?" *His wife left him because she felt she couldn't get ahead and stay married to him*, Eileen thought. He shot her a ruthless look as if sensing she was about to evade the question. "Be honest."

Heart pounding at the brooding intensity on his face, she admitted honestly, "I would like the prestige, the additional responsibility, and challenge. The truth of the matter is, I never realized how ambitious I was until Ted died and I had to support myself. Even loving you, that much about me hasn't changed, Ross. I need to work. I need that validation of self-worth, the assurance that I can succeed on my own, which I get from doing my work."

His inscrutable attitude was all the more unnerving. "I can understand that," he said carefully. "I can't imagine myself not working, either. But as for the commuting—I've lived alone for a long time, Eileen. I know what it's like, from my dealings with my son, to be a 'weekend father.' I don't want that again. I don't want it for Teddy. I don't want it for myself. More specifically, I don't want to be without you. Scheduling time alone together the past few months has been hard enough. If we were to attempt this long-distance romance, either married or not...." His jaw tightened, his expression becoming hard and resentful.

"That sounds like an ultimatum," she shot back angrily. Dammit, she'd worked hard for this. Illogical as it was, she had wanted—almost expected—him to be happy for her.

"I don't mean it to be," he said tiredly. "And I am proud of you, happy for your professional success and what this offer means." He paused. The unhappy look on his face told her he was remembering, searching into his past. Abruptly, his attitude gentled. He glanced at her, maintaining a reasonable tone with obvious effort. "I won't try and stop you from accepting the position in Gary. The offer to marry me still stands, whatever you decide. And if you really want to take it, we'll try and work it out." His weary tone told her he wasn't betting odds on the success of such an endeavor.

Eileen sighed, pressing both hands over eyes that were burning with weariness. She knew he wasn't just giving lip service to what she wanted to hear. If the position in Gary was what she truly wanted, he would sincerely try to make it work. But he was right about one thing—it wasn't a good beginning for a marriage. Unexpectedly, his hand covered hers, transmitting his warmth and affection and even his understanding. Remembering the boundless joy and love he had given her over the past months, she was desperate for peace between them. Yet there were no simple solutions. And she couldn't deny she did want to move further up the career ladder. They sat in silence for several minutes. "What are you going to do about the job?" he asked finally, his voice the softest caress.

She shook her head, feeling all at once helplessly close to bursting into tears again. The timing was so rotten. "I don't know." She looked at him imploringly. "I promised them an answer by the end of the week."

He made a stabbing attempt to inject a light touch into the exchange. "Well, don't rush into anything. Think it through carefully, list the pros and the cons. I don't want to lose you, Eileen." He was willing to compromise after all, although it still wasn't the primrose path he would have chosen. Eileen sighed.

"Thank you for being so good to me," she said.

There was a heart-stopping pause. More than ever, she needed to be taken into his arms and simply held, assured everything would be all right, that they could find a way to work it out. Aware of the restaurant crowd around them, he leaned back in his chair to survey her thoughtfully.

"I do love you," he said quietly.

"I know," she responded. That was what made it so hard.

JANEY EXPRESSED A SIMILAR RESERVE when Eileen told her. They were sitting in her kitchen. The baby was on her lap. The boys were swimming with the teenage twins in the backyard pool, and distant yells and splashing sounds could be heard above the soft lull of the indoor fan.

"There will be other jobs at other banks, Eileen," Janey said, handing the baby a soft pretzel stick. "Even if your present job doesn't work out. Will there ever be another man you love as much as Ross Mitchell?"

"Is it that obvious?" Eileen, looking miserable, stirred her tea.

Her older sister smiled sympathetically, recounting dryly, "Before Ross came along, you would have jumped at the chance for promotion in a minute, no matter what was involved. The fact that you're reluctant to accept such validation of your success ought to tell you something."

"It does. And I do love him. But the idea of being dependent on any man scares me to death." She glanced up, her brow furrowed. "What will happen to me and Teddy if Ross dies, or if the marriage doesn't work out. What then? I can't go through that agony of insecurity again. I have to be prepared this time. I can't jump into marriage blindly again. And no matter what Ross says, Teddy is my responsibility. I've got to put him through college...."

"Ross would do that for you," Janey counseled quietly.

"Yes, but I want to do it. It makes me happy providing for Teddy. And I don't want to just do it marginally. I want him to be proud of me. I want to be proud of myself. I want to know I've been the best businesswoman I could possibly be, no holds barred, no excuses given."

"I understand that. I feel the same way about being a homemaker," Janey concurred. "And eventually, when the children are grown, I'll probably go back to work in some capacity, too, for the same satisfaction."

"So where does that leave me now?" Glumly, Eileen rested her chin on her fist.

"You know there are no guarantees in life," Janey pointed out pragmatically. "As for your security, you can still have that by continuing to work after you're married. Ross will support that wholeheartedly. It's your abandoning him by moving to another city he won't support in his heart. And face it, after what he went through with his first wife, he shouldn't have to."

"But don't you see that by compromising I'd be shortchanging myself?" Eileen said.

"That's what marriage is all about...compromise," Janey said gently. "If you really love Ross as much as you say, you'll find a way to be together and satisfy your need to achieve professionally, too."

"You say that as if it were as simple as ABC," Eileen grumbled.

"It isn't, but then in the end nothing in life that's worth anything is," she pointed out with finality.

In the next twenty-four hours Eileen mentally played every possible solution to her dilemma. She imagined them delaying their wedding, marrying anyway, then moving—terrible! She considered marrying and commuting. No alternative that promised complete career happiness and upward mobility provided her with anything even closely resembling personal happiness. Realizing that her older sister had been right again, Eileen followed the dictate of her heart.

"I've made a decision." Eileen faced Ross nervously late the next evening. She'd arranged for a sitter for Teddy and met Ross at his house. She could only hope he would be pleased.

"What is it?" His expression was tense but receptive. She sensed he had girded himself to make whatever adjustments were necessary. And the fact he was so willing to compromise made her heart soar.

"I'm turning the offer down." She was a bundle of nerves. Her hands were shaking, her knees weak. Yet her resolve was firm.

Ross remained carefully impassive, not reacting with the joy she had expected. Her spirits sank and he frowned even more, stepping closer. "How much part did I play in your decision?" He tilted his head to study her better, as if looking for the slightest hint of dishonesty. He did not want her to martyr herself on his behalf.

She grinned, finally at peace with her decision. Janey was right—with Ross at her side, everything else would just fall into place. And if not, she'd eventually make it work. "Just about everything." There was no reason to be coy. She wanted him to know the depth of her love.

Relief relaxed the lines of his face. He spoke in an odd, yet tender tone. "Do you resent me for wanting you to stay?" For a second he seemed barely to breathe.

"I understand you can't move your law practice." And with the position only a temporary one, it would be foolish of him to attempt it. Hence, the burden fell on her. Sensing he needed some further reassurance, though, she said, "But to be blunt, no, you weren't the *only* reason. Just the main one. I had Teddy to consider, too. I think it would be too difficult for him, moving twice and adjusting to having us married. I want him to be secure. I want him to have the benefits of your love full time. And I want it for myself." She felt elated by her new objectivity.

"I want that, too," Ross said sincerely, his voice deep and vibrant with emotion. He closed the distance between them with slow, leisurely strides. "I love you, Eileen." He wrapped her in a fierce hug.

His lips moved just below her ear, lingered at her temple, her cheek.

"I love you, too," Eileen murmured throatily. Everything that had been wrong with her world righted as she felt the security of his arms around her, and suddenly she knew that everything truly was going to be all right again. And as for her disappointment at having to give up the job, well, somehow they would work that out, too, given time. She would just have to find another way to succeed professionally.

He kissed her eloquently, his eager tongue caressing her mouth, tantalizing sweetly. It was a kiss for her ravaged soul to melt into. Her thoughts spun out, her emotions whirled and gentled as his hands moved down her back to her hips, then cupped her against him fiercely until she matched his own lusty, unsated needs. His tormented groan was a heady invitation, and when they'd finished, she was curled into the strength of his body, her hands clasping his shoulders, so dizzy she could barely stand. Love flowed renewed within her like warm honey, and happiness spun around her like ethereal threads. Palms on his forearms, she tilted her face to his, secure enough again to tease lightly, "Listen, Mr. Mitchell, if that marriage proposal still stands—"

"Woman, that's one promise I am holding you to for better or for worse." He kissed her again ardently. Then, contentment and peace flowing between them, he excused himself temporarily and returned posthaste to hand her a calendar and pen. "Just pick a date." His dark brows arched mischievously. His eyes were compelling as he laced his hands possessively around her waist. "But do me a favor and make it soon."

"I wouldn't have it any other way," she murmured approvingly.

After much deliberation and consulting of mutual work schedules, they finally decided on August 1 for the wedding. Teddy would be ring bearer, and Janey and Hugh would host the small private ceremony in their backyard. Eileen and Ross would take Teddy for his annual visit to Ted's parents, and the honeymoon would be in nearby Miami and the Florida Keys. Before returning to Indianapolis, Teddy, Eileen and Ross would all meet Steve in Bermuda, and the four of them would spend a few additional days together.

THE MOST PRESSING PROBLEM was combining homes. "I'm beginning to regret my decision to move in here," Eileen said several weeks later, facing the mountain of paraphernalia Ross had stored in two of the extra upstairs bedrooms.

"What can I tell you?" He shrugged helplessly. "Keep sorting." In his gray sweatshirt and cutoff jeans, he passed by her with a load of boxes in his arms. He nodded toward the stack of worn spiral notebooks and clothes. "Most of that stuff is a holdover from my law-school days. I'll want to keep the texts. The notes we can put in my old metal filing cabinets down in the basement. The clothes—well, the clothes you'll probably have to give to charity."

"If they'll take them," she said, holding up a ragged tie-dyed undershirt that was now hopelessly out of date.

"Very funny." He sent her a mock reproachful glare. "Better watch it or you'll prompt me to see how it looks on you!"

"Ho, ho, counselor," she shot back in the same teasing gibe.

Sighing wearily, Eileen stacked his notebooks neatly in an empty carton. Nearby was a carefully preserved Cincinnati Bengals pennant beside a small men's orange-and-black sweatshirt, still in its plastic wrapping.

"Oh, damn. I meant to take those to Steve." Ross put down his boxes and stepped over to clear a space on a bureau. "Just put those gifts here, for the time being. Along with anything else you find that you think Steve might want."

"Didn't your mother ever teach you not to rearrange the junk?" she asked.

"No!" Ross retorted good-humoredly, heading out to the kitchen.

She heaved an enormous sigh. "You're a wonderful lawyer, Ross, and a fine outstanding member of the community," she murmured to herself. "Even your biceps are magnificent." Not to mention his lovemaking. "But you keep too much damn stuff!" She had fallen in love with a superhero and discovered him to be a closet pack rat! She smiled at the imagery evoked, not really all that upset about his sloppiness. His untidy streak only made him seem more human, more real.

Eileen tossed out a yellowing three-year-old copy of the Indianapolis Sunday newspaper. Unexpectedly, beneath that she discovered a photo album. Eileen put it aside and picked up a fat manila envelope. She glanced inside. Noting some snapshots, she started to close it, then stopped, as her gaze caught on a headful of tousled white-blond hair. *Teddy!* she thought, amazed. Curiosity led her to pull the photos out, then shock made her lean against the bureau weakly. It might have been Teddy standing beside a much younger Ross—a Ross in his mid-twenties.

Ross appeared in the door. His face whitened at the pallor of hers. He started forward as warily as if defusing a time bomb. "What are you looking at?"

She held up a picture for his perusal. "Who is this?" In her heart, she felt she already knew.

His jaw clenched. He swallowed, then sighed. "Steve."

The room took on the blur of unreality, much as it would if she were going to faint at any second. With effort, she retained her surface composure. "Do you realize how much he looked like Teddy?" Her voice was icy with hurt. When he said nothing and merely continued to stare at her in the same numb way, her gaze returned to the pictures. Both boys had the same deep tan, hair color and thick-lashed gaze. But it was their smile that got to her. Something so innocent and trusting and yet little-boy devilish all at once. Even the way they held their lips seemed the same. It was Teddy through and through—and yet it was not.

She flipped through the rest of the photos, encountering vivid color snapshots of Ross and Steve fishing together, boating, even playing ball. She swallowed hard. "So this is what Steve looked like when he was younger, about Teddy's age right now." She laughed, sounding faintly hysterical, even to her own ears. "It's funny, isn't it? Almost spooky. They've even got the same body language." And then suddenly it wasn't funny at all.

"Yes, their coloring is the same, or almost," Ross confirmed quietly.

"It's more than that." She cut off his protest.

It was eerie, but not unheard of, or even unexperienced by her, this phenomenon of two children, unrelated by blood, looking alike. She thought of the look-alikes for former President Carter and film star Robert Redford and Jacqueline Onassis. But never, ever had she encountered anything so close to home—to her son. Or been in a position where someone she loved could replace someone else's loss. Ross had lost daily contact with his son Steve when he and his wife had divorced. He had even lamented to Eileen the lack of contact with Steve, the years he had lost.

"You did notice how much alike our sons are, at least at the age of nine?" Would Teddy be as tall and slim, bronzed and dark-blond as Steve when he got older, she wondered. Would he be as lanky and clumsy, despite the exterior polish in terms of clothes and haircuts as Steve was now at fourteen?

Ross nodded. "Yes. Does it bother you so much?" He put the envelope of photos aside and moved to step forward, but she blocked his approach with outstretched palms. She didn't want to be physically close to him, not yet. "Why didn't you tell me?" Her throat was tight.

"I don't know. I didn't think it was relevant." Ross looked sick. There was a faint bead of perspiration on his upper lip. He uttered a shaky laugh. "At first there was no sane way to work it into the conversation. What was I suppose to say? 'Hello, Ms Garrett, I met your son the other day, and believe me it was like seeing a ghost.' No, no way. You resented my interference enough as it was. Later, I thought you might object for the same emotional reasons you're experiencing now. It was too bizarre. I couldn't risk it—there was too much at stake. I liked Teddy—I wanted him to play on my team. I wanted to know you. And if you knew how much he looked like Steve at that same age, you would have suspected my motives."

Tears streamed down her face. Her fists were clenched tight at her sides. "So you lied to me."

He winced as if he'd been struck. "I just didn't mention it. For all I knew the resemblance could have been my imagination—the wishful thinking of a father who missed his son."

How exactly correct, she thought. *And how frightening.* Was that all Teddy was to him—a chance to make up for Ross's enforced distance from Stephen? "The first day you came to see me," she ground out, "you said you had an instant rapport with Teddy. Was this resemblance one of the reasons? Was it the main reason, the only reason?" Her voice rose hysterically.

He countered with absolute calm. His gaze was so intense it chilled her to her soul. How very reasonable he was, how collected. She wondered obliquely how many times he had already been through this ugly scenario in his mind, prepared for it.

"Maybe, partially, at the very first, that is what attracted me to him. But the boy was crying out for love, Eileen—love only a man could give."

"Thanks for the compliment." Bitterness choked her every word.

He stiffened defensively. "I don't mean to hurt you, but it's true," Ross shot back angrily. "Teddy hungered for what you couldn't and never will be able to give him—the empathy, love and guidance of another man. For heaven's sake, the boy was so desperate for male attention he faked a fall into an unlit pool."

And Ross had dived in unselfishly after him, in an effort to save Teddy's life. She blanched, remembering. She would have forgiven him at that moment had he not looked so arrogantly judgmental. Her temper flared hotly in response, and before she could stop herself the words poured out. "Just why was it you were able to react so unselfishly and swiftly that night, Ross? Did you think you were rescuing your son or mine?" Once the words were out, she could hardly believe she'd been that cruel, but she knew from the stricken look on his face she'd hurt him deeply.

He looked, at that moment, as if it were taking every bit of self-control not to strike her. "I knew damn well who Teddy was at the time." The words were grated out between clenched teeth.

She wanted to believe him, but she couldn't dismiss his obvious lie of omission. She took several deep breaths, trying to get a grip on her emotions. Finally, she admitted more reasonably, "All right, I can understand why you didn't tell me at first. That would have been difficult. But why not in Bermuda after I'd met Stephen and grown to like him, and he me? Why did you keep something as important as this from me?" It came to her then that Ted had kept things from her too—his growing dependence on alcohol, the other women who fleetingly consoled his sagging ego. Was she making the same type of mistake, only under different circumstances? Was she blinding herself to reality again? Her heart said no, but her mind was uncertain.

"Because I didn't want you to think I was marrying you just for that reason." He stepped around the boxes, and pinned her there in his arms. She resisted, whipping her head to the side to avoid his kiss. His mouth hovered above hers for one yearning instant, then drew back in wordless defeat.

She felt the pain and longing so acutely she nearly cried out. Bitterness swamped her. She recalled too well the failure she had been as Ted's wife. "You really expect me to believe you want me for myself?" Would Ross ever have looked at her if it hadn't been for Teddy, and the fact that he'd lost custody and contact with his own son at the same stage in the boy's development?

"Yes, Eileen—"

She broke away from him, and more tears fell, blinding her to everything else but her own pain. "God, I can't believe this is happening to me." She pressed a hand against her mouth to stifle the sobs welling up in her throat. "I gave up a job, a promotion, for this!" It was the worst possible thing she could have said. He reacted as if he'd been stabbed. Yet she couldn't stop the flow of painful words. "All this time it was Teddy you wanted, not me. That's why you opposed that job so vehemently, why you didn't want to wait a year. What were you thinking, Ross? That raising Teddy would make up for all the years you missed with your own son?" She flung one of his old spiral notebooks at him. He ducked adroitly, and it crashed to the floor, papers flying every which way.

He approached slowly, an inch at a time, his hands balled at his sides. "Maybe. Your son needs a father, Eileen."

"So does yours. But that didn't mean you were there for him, did it?" she shouted, pacing back and forth in the cluttered room. She whirled toward him defiantly. "What happens when you realize once and for all Teddy is not Stephen? Will you desert us, too? Or just force me—through neglect or by holding me back professionally—to leave you, too?" They were the most merciless words she could have spoken. She knew it, but could not control it, any more than she could direct the events that had brought them to this place.

He faced her in exasperation. "You know I'd never leave you, Eileen. And as for holding you back—" The words came with difficulty. "I would never deliberately do that, either."

"Haven't you already, by your refusal to support my promotion?"

He said nothing, his pallor increasing.

Realizing she couldn't take much more, she whirled frenetically and pivoted toward the door, stumbling as she tripped over a carton. "Where are you going?" Ross caught up with her in three long strides. Grabbing her arm, he swung her around to face him.

She fought to extricate herself from his grip, failed. "Home. Where I belong!"

He blocked her path. "I know you're upset, therefore I'll forgive you for everything you've said, because I know in your heart you didn't mean it. But what I won't forget is your leaving me, now, at the time I need you to stay with me the most. When I need you to be here and hash this out and work through our problems."

"Our problems or yours?" she interrupted haughtily, resenting the fact that she couldn't break his hold on her even though he was not physically harming her and never would.

"Ours." His tone was flat, final. "If you leave me now, this is it," he threatened, very low. "I don't want another runaway wife. And I couldn't bear to lose a son again. And despite what you think, I consider Teddy to be just that. But not because of his looks—because of the person he is inside."

Tears flowed down her cheeks. Didn't he understand how betrayed she felt?

"I understand the resemblance between the boys is a problem for you. It was for me, too, initially. But we can work it out." He was soothing and calm, while her fury was still burning through her.

Blinded by her tears, she stormed from his home without a backward glance. She had to think—and

she knew her mind was clouded by doubts and disappointment. Even so, a part of her hoped he'd come
after her. But he did nothing to stop her—nothing at
all.

11

JANEY WATCHED EILEEN preparing for the movers, disapproval clearly etched on her face. "You're making a mistake," she counseled sternly, not bothering to disguise the exasperation in her voice.

"If the bank was good enough to reconsider me for a job I'd already turned down, the least I can do is accept it," Eileen countered. It had been tough, going back to the bank manager, hat in hand, but in the end she felt she had done what was best for all of them.

"You're running away," Janey emphasized.

The living room was strewn with boxes, and Eileen identified the contents of another cardboard carton with black magic marker. "Precisely why I'm leaving. Ross wants and needs a woman who will stay with him through thick and thin. I couldn't. End of story. I had my chance and I blew it."

"You still love Ross. No matter where you live or how much distance you put between you and him, that will never change. Your feelings won't just dry up and go away." Janey continued to trail her sister from chore to chore.

"Yes, I do love him, and I don't expect my feelings for him to disappear." She knew they never would. She loved Ross more deeply than she had ever loved any man. "But that doesn't change what happened between us. Face it, he can't bring himself to forgive me."

"Has he told you that specifically?"

"He doesn't have to. Look, he told me when I walked out that door that if I left that was it. I was angry and upset." She swallowed hard and shoved a hand through her hair. "I guess maybe in my heart I didn't believe him. I thought—I thought he'd always have a place for me in his heart, that he'd be able to forgive me, that he'd see I needed time to think, to make sure that Ted's deceptions wouldn't be repeated—in any form—with him. Evidently, that's not the case." She gave her sister a wry smile. "He hasn't called or tried to talk to me once."

"Have you tried to see him, to explain?"

The first forty-eight hours after their fight she'd called several times, then lost her nerve and hung up at the last minute. But rather than go into all that with her sister again, she placed her hands on her hips and shot back, "It wouldn't do any good. Face it, dear heart, he's lost that 'romantic gleam' in his eyes. Now that he knows the true shallowness of my character he couldn't care less what happens to me or my son." Either that or he had been involved with her for all the wrong reasons, as she'd hot-temperedly asserted. It wasn't a possibility she wanted to pursue, either in thought or discussion with Janey, so she fell silent.

"You're being stubborn and shortsighted!" Janey shot back. Abruptly, she softened. "Think about Teddy."

"You don't have to remind me how much he's been hurt. I haven't talked to Steve, but I would imagine Ross's son feels the same way. They were looking forward to getting acquainted, to being a real family."

"It could still happen," Janey pointed out gently.

Eileen knew nothing would make Teddy happier.

In fact, being the eternal optimist he was, he still hadn't given up hope that she and Ross would eventually get back together. And admittedly, at odd moments she found herself hoping unconsciously, too. But she couldn't, in good conscience, foster false hope for any of them.

Sighing, she reiterated with false calm, "Look, Janey, do me a favor and face the facts. Ross and I were getting married for all the wrong reasons. Obviously, I didn't know Ross any more than I knew Ted. And look what happened when Ted and I married. It was a disaster."

"You were a child when you married Ted, barely out of your teens."

A sardonic smile tugged at the corner of Eileen's mouth as she recalled how hysterically she'd reacted when she'd found out about the resemblance between Steve and Teddy. "Sometimes I don't feel much more grown-up now."

Her sister's gaze narrowed reproachfully. "Maybe if you'd quit acting like such a child, you could work things out." Eileen shook her head, then stepped around her. Wordlessly, she scribbled on the top of another box, denoting kitchen utensils and tableware inside. Janey balled her fists. "Damn it, Eileen, so you're scared. Everyone has prewedding jitters."

Eileen laughed hollowly, shoving a shock of golden-brown hair from her eyes. There were dark circles beneath her eyes. Even makeup couldn't conceal her washed-out look or disguise the hopelessness she felt in her heart. "Is that all you think this is?" It felt like the end of her life.

"Frankly, yes." More gently, Janey soothed, "It's still not too late to rectify the situation, you know. You could go to Ross, talk to him, ask him to give you more time."

Despair brought tears to her eyes. "You didn't see Ross's face when I walked out on him. He said he didn't want another runaway wife, that if I went it would be over."

"He didn't mean it."

Eileen sat down heavily on the chesterfield. "That was three weeks ago. He hasn't called since."

"Who can blame him? You've been going miles out of your way to avoid him."

Only because I've been afraid to face him, Eileen admitted to herself. "I was at the softball game the other night," she reminded her older sister stubbornly. It had been the last one Teddy would play in. Ross had been right, his team was destined for league championship—with or without her son. It was Teddy who was miserably disappointed at having to quit now, when he'd already gone so far with his winning group. "If he had wanted to see me or talk to me, he had his chance."

"Did he?" There was no quarter in Janey's tone. Scathingly, she continued, "Yes, you were at the game, Eileen, but you spent the whole time sitting next to two other single male parents. Do you think Ross didn't notice you were cosseted neatly between two eligible men?"

She lifted her shoulders in a defiant shrug. So maybe she had wanted to make Ross jealous. After all, he had given her that damn inscrutable glare of his, the one where she felt she was being dissected bit by bit. "They did talk to me first."

"And you didn't want to be rude," Janey rejoined dryly, predicting what was to be her kid sister's next excuse. "Come on, Eileen, I saw you. You were encouraging them."

Eileen's conscience made her blush, but her tone was cool. "Maybe a little."

"A lot."

She'd hoped Ross would be jealous. She'd wanted him to claim her, caveman style. It hadn't worked out that way. He'd behaved as if she hadn't existed, and she'd left the park more dejected than before, feeling especially guilty for having used the other men. That wasn't like her. But come to think of it, nothing she'd done lately was.

"Why don't you call him?" Janey asked again. When Eileen didn't reply, Janey asked, "Honestly, Eileen, after all the two of you shared together, how can you not try just one more time to salvage something from your affair?"

Eileen went back to inspecting the numbered cartons, making sure they were ready for the movers. "Because Teddy would be hurt again if it didn't work out."

"He doesn't ever have to know. I'll take him home with me."

Eileen vacillated. She wanted to see Ross, she knew she did.

Janey recognized her weakness and pounced on it. "Getting back together with Ross would be the best action you could ever take, for yourself, your son, for Steve, and for Ross. You can't leave without talking to Ross."

Eileen swallowed. "I just don't want to make everything worse."

"You won't. Believe me, you won't. You've both had plenty of time to cool off. If you both weren't so stubborn, you'd have patched this misunderstanding up by now."

"Maybe." Eileen knew Ross was as careful of Teddy's feelings as she was. Maybe, just maybe, he was feeling a similar reluctance. "And while you're at it, apologize for the other night." Janey propelled her inside, toward the phone. When Eileen started to protest that she still had a million things to do, her sister ordered, "Dial, girl. Now."

With a last emphatic look, Janey disappeared. Eileen stood there in the deserted hall, looking down at the phone. It was now or never. What did she have to lose except her pride, and most of that seemed vanquished already.

Ross's secretary put Eileen on hold, and then, after a lengthy pause, came back on the line and reluctantly reported that Ross was in conference and couldn't be disturbed. Eileen knew a business lie when she heard one. Politely, she left a brief message, thanking Ross for helping Teddy polish his softball skills, and then sadly hung up the phone. It really was over between them, then. She'd never been so miserable in her life.

THAT NIGHT Teddy went with Janey to spend the evening with his cousins while Eileen vacuumed all the living room and part of the upstairs hall. Finally, when her sweeper quit, she sat on the top stairs and began to cry. She'd made such a mess of everything. Nothing in her life seemed to work anymore. "Hell's bells, I give up."

"You shouldn't. Not until you've exhausted every chance of a permanent repair." Ross stood framed in the doorway. Eileen's head lifted at the familiar tone. Despite her misgivings, joy flooded her heart and tears shone in her eyes. She had missed that big lug more than she'd ever thought possible. Even his gentle sarcasm was a welcome balm to her heart. His eyes caught hers and held. Never had she seen a more welcome smile.

"Generally speaking, appliances respond to kindness, too." There were two medium-sized cardboard boxes in his hands. Walking in, Ross shut the door with a gentle prod of his foot and set the boxes down. "Where's Teddy?"

"At Janey's. He's spending the night."

"Good. What I have to say is strictly between us."

That sounded ominous. Needing to delay what she was sure was going to be bad news, she asked quickly, "What's in the boxes?"

He gestured as if the matter were of supreme unimportance. "Just a few items of mine I want you to see when you have the time to go through them." Clearly, he had other actions planned. A slender delicate thread of understanding began to form between them. Like a lifeline to safety and love it towed them gently, inevitably, closer.

"I thought it was all over between us," she gulped. "You said—"

"I know what I said when you walked out the door," he said gruffly. The air around them was electric with their suppressed need. A muscle worked tautly in his jaw. He stalked closer, shaking his head in an exasperated bemusement that was directed at himself as much as her. "Don't you think I haven't regretted it à thousand times? But I wasn't sure you would be able to forgive me for holding out on you."

"But the past three weeks," she sputtered. "All those days and nights—"

"I knew you needed some time alone to think. All I wanted was a sign there was still a chance." He sighed. A glimmer of the pain he'd felt showed on his face.

He'd wanted hope, and she'd responded with a retaliatory flirtation with other men. "I didn't mean to make you angry," she whispered tremulously.

"The hell you didn't!" he growled. A rueful smile curved his lips into a handsome smile. "But you did, and it started me thinking, and I haven't stopped since." Unexpectedly, his glance fell to the tangle of machinery at her feet. "The vacuum giving you trouble again?" he asked.

She nodded, for a moment not trusting herself to speak. "I guess I need a man around the house after all." A thousand vibrant emotions spun through her, none of which she was ashamed to share.

He shot her a tolerantly teasing look. "Anyone special in mind?"

"Only you." Her voice was so quiet she thought for a second he hadn't deciphered what she had said. But a moment later he had pulled her to her feet and was holding her against him, raining hot damp kisses over her face, across her mouth, down her neck. "You're a lot of trouble, Eileen Garrett." He straightened, pulling back enough so she could look deep into his eyes. "But you're worth it." His nearness made her senses spin.

Without warning, his attention returned to the malfunctioning machine. "Want me to take a look?"

"Later, and only if you wouldn't mind." Now that he was here again, she didn't want to share his attention with anything else.

"I don't mind," he said softly, kissing her again. "But you're right. At the moment I can think of better, more urgent things to do." Bending, he kissed her again and then again. "I'm sorry I didn't take your call this afternoon," he said softly, threading his fingers through the mussed ends of her hair, gently smoothing the tangled silk. "I was in."

So she'd been right, that excuse was a business lie! Moving away from him, she looked down at her hands, twisting them nervously together. His arms on her shoulders, he tenderly turned her to face him, then cupped a hand under her chin, continuing seriously, "I knew what we had to say couldn't be said over the phone. But before we met I wanted to end every bit of mystery between us once and for all. That's what is in the boxes. My life history, from birth forward." At her astonished look, he continued, "You wanted to know what else you were missing. Well, that's it. I'm all yours for the rest of the night, or as long as you'll let me stay," he said softly. Stunned, she sat down. "I'll answer any and every question you have," Ross continued soothingly. "I'll tell you everything and anything you want to know as long as you love me and keep on loving me and never quit."

"I do and I will!" she cried, her heart filling with relief.

"Good enough." He moved closer to sit next to her on the stairs, his thigh almost, but not quite, touching hers. An ache started in her middle and spread languorously throughout her entire body. How she needed to be held by him again, and to embrace him to her.

"Where do you want to begin?" Ross continued in a steely, determined voice.

She pivoted toward him, and twined her fingertips with his, lifting her face to meet his. "How about here?" She touched his fingertips to her lips. Emotion clogged her throat, making the last word barely above a whisper. "Peace?"

"Peace," he agreed.

Bravely, she took a deep breath and plunged on, wanting him to know how she felt. "I was never that angry with you, Ross. Just scared. I had such great expectations the last time I married. It was happening all over again, only the feelings were one hundred times more moving and powerful than they were with Ted. I was constantly elated. Just the sound of your voice could make me smile. I wanted you with me all the time and when you weren't I was just miserable, marking time until we were together. Add to that the fact you made Teddy deliriously happy and understood him in man-to-man ways that I never will be able to. You gave me security, hope for the future. In short, our relationship was everything I'd ever dreamed come true, and it terrified me. I was afraid I wanted too much again. I was afraid I was being unrealistic, blind to the reality of what marriage would no doubt turn out to be. I was scared my expectations wouldn't be met or worse, that I wouldn't please you and that I wouldn't be able to handle it well if it didn't work out.''

"And how do you feel now?" he asked.

"The same. Still scared." But she was willing to take the risk, if only he was. She waited for him to say something, anything.

He rose and began walking down the stairs. "I'm apprehensive, too." At the foot of the stairs, he turned to face her. "I wasn't exactly a pro at marriage before, either, you know. And more than anything I wanted you to be happy. If that meant loving you enough to let you go—" He swallowed as if unable to go on, shook his head. She knew then he'd been as miserable and uncertain as she. The knowledge was reassuring in a way that made her heart soar. But she had some explaining of her own to do yet.

She rose to join him at the landing. "About the other night at the softball game—"

His eyes sparkled with unchecked amusement. "I know a ploy to make me jealous when I see one," he growled reprovingly. Clearly, if she tried a similar tactic again he would not be so forgiving.

"Then why didn't you react?" she asked as she joined him on the ground floor.

"And let you think it had worked? Woman, you don't know much about the male psyche." He pressed her gently back onto the carpeted stairs. "However, for the record, if you ever do it again—"

"Yes?" she questioned teasingly between passionate kisses.

"I'll be forced to resort to my most macho act. I'll carry you off, caveman style. And then I'll do this—" his hand caressed the uppermost swell of her breast "—and this—" his palm glided over her ribs and dipped low into the waistband of her pants "—and this—" his fingertips trailed lower, to gently caress the sensitive inside of her thighs, "until you're breathless with longing and begging me for the release only I can give." She was tingling all over right now, and he gazed down into her face, lovingly memorizing every detail. "And then—" He sighed, the warmth of his breath teasing the silken hair at her temples.

"What?" Contentment flowed through her. Anticipation made the blood pulse wildly through her veins.

"Then I'll leave." Implacably he sat up, defending his honor. Not about to let him get away with such a ploy, she swiftly pulled him back down by the edges of his shirt.

"That's mean!" Her tone was strident and complaining.

He grinned, mischievously raising and lowering his brows. "Yes, but it will teach you not to tease."

"It already has." She sighed. She playfully assumed a pose of surrender, which instantly had the desired affect.

"Does that mean I have permission to continue? Why don't we move to the comfort of the floor?" he grinned. His mouth teased the line of her cheekbone. His tongue tantalized the inner shell of her ear.

She basked in his sensual attention, running her hands exploringly up and over the rounded swell of his biceps, over the curve of his shoulders to the strongly muscled back. "Permission? You have my whole-hearted support. In fact, I know a few moves of my own." She demonstrated with long passionate kisses and deliberate caresses. Soon, aching with desire, they lay together, their love a tangible essence between them, both of them trembling in sweetest anticipation.

"Oh, love," he murmured against the fragrant tumble of her hair, "I've missed you."

"I've missed you, too." She sighed.

His lips dipped to hers, savoring the softness she offered. Ardently, she traced patterns in the swirls of chest hair, clasped the backs of his thighs and applied soft upward pressure until he moved, eager and ready, against her. She welcomed the pressure of his weight, the tumultuous joining, the floating love-weighted descent to peace. A steamy interval later, when their breathing had slowed to a more manageable rate, they lay together, arms and legs entwined. "So what are we going to do next?" Eileen asked. There was nothing more gladdening than the steady strong beat of his heart, or the feel of his arms around her, holding her close.

"Why not get married as planned?" he suggested lightly. "I have it on good authority that Janey never canceled the order for the cake or the minister. And we took care of the license weeks ago. It's still valid. My house, believe it or not, is completely cleaned and organized and ready for you and Teddy to move in. It'd be simple enough for the movers to transfer your belongings there. And we could take Teddy down to Florida and see his grandparents as planned, then swing on over to have a reunion with Steve."

It was what she'd been wishing for all along, but her situation at the bank was more of a problem. She sighed with dismay against his chest. "What about my job?" Eileen asked.

He threaded his fingers through her hair, massaging slowly. "That, darling, is more of a quandary. If you want to take the position, just for the year, I could handle the commute. I don't want to hold you back. But I'd still want to get married."

Any qualms she might have had about Ross returning to his more youthful, admittedly chauvinistic thinking faded. She propped her chin up on her bent elbow and looked him squarely in the face, needing to get his reaction. "Actually, I've been thinking about going back to school for my MBA," she said tentatively, wanting him to approve. More than anything, she wanted to make him as happy as he had made her. "Do you think you could handle a student wife, just for a year or two?"

His hands clasped low on her back, holding her possessively close. "I'll take you any way I can get you."

"I'm interested in a half-time, two-year program. It's designed for people who work or are otherwise occupied—women who have children at home—many of them have infants." She stressed the last word. The possibility of having another child had been in her mind more and more.

Speculative interest lit up his eyes. "Are you suggesting what I think you are?"

She nodded, stretching against his prone length.

"How do you think the boys would react?" Ross queried tentatively.

"I don't think either Steve or Teddy would mind. In fact, I think they'd welcome an addition to our blended family as long as we're together," she assured him.

"I'll second that." He sighed. "How soon do you think we can begin working on it?" His warmth seared her skin, his tongue teased her nape. He caught her against him, his mouth warm and compelling, savoring each tender caress.

"How about tomorrow night, as soon as it's legal?" She grinned a breathless time later. "In the mean-time—" she feathered butterfly kisses down his chest "—I guess a little pregame warm-up wouldn't hurt. Would it, coach?"

He caught her to him ardently and moved so she was beneath him, his arm cushioning her neck. The tip of his tongue stroked the tangy sweetness of her lower lip until she was powerless to resist him, excitement coursing through her body like golden bubbles of champagne. He murmured softly, bending over her, his eyes reflecting his love, "Anything for our home team...."

EYE OF THE STORM

MAURA SEGER

A powerful portrayal of the events of World War II in the Pacific, *Eye of the Storm* is a riveting story of how love triumphs over hatred. In this, the first of a three book chronicle, Army nurse Maggie Lawrence meets Marine Sgt. Anthony Gargano. Despite military regulations against fraternization, they resolve to face together whatever lies ahead.... Also known by her fans as Laurel Winslow, Sara Jennings, Anne MacNeil and Jenny Bates, Maura Seger, author of this searing novel, was named by ROMANTIC TIMES as 1984's Most Versatile Romance Author.

At your favorite bookstore in March.

EYE-B-1

The Fourth
Harlequin American Romance
Premier Edition

GENTLY INTO NIGHT

KATHERINE COFFARO

Emily Ruska and Joel Kline
are two New York City police detectives
caught between conflicting values
and an undeniable attraction
for each other.

Exclusive Harlequin home subscriber benefits!

- SPECIAL LOW PRICES for home subscribers only
- CONVENIENCE of home delivery
- NO CHARGE for postage and handling
- FREE *Harlequin Romance Digest®*
- FREE BONUS books
- NEW TITLES 2 months ahead of retail
- MEMBER of the largest romance fiction book club in the world

Enter a uniquely exciting new world with

Harlequin American Romance T.M.

Harlequin American Romances are the first romances to explore today's love relationships. These compelling novels reach into the hearts and minds of women across America... probing the most intimate moments of romance, love and desire.

You'll follow romantic heroines and irresistible men as they boldly face confusing choices. Career first, love later? Love without marriage? Long-distance relationships? All the experiences that make love real are captured in the tender, loving pages of **Harlequin American Romances.**

What makes American women so different when it comes to love? Find out with **Harlequin American Romance!**

Send for your introductory FREE book now!

Get this book FREE!

Mail to:
Harlequin Reader Service

In the U.S.
2504 West Southern Ave.
Tempe, AZ 85282

In Canada
P.O. Box 2800, Postal Station A
5170 Yonge St., Willowdale, Ont. M2N 5T5

YES! I want to be one of the first to discover
Harlequin American Romance. Send me FREE and without obligation *Twice in a Lifetime.* If you do not hear from me after I have examined my FREE book, please send me the 4 new **Harlequin American Romances** each month as soon as they come off the presses. I understand that I will be billed only $2.25 for each book (total $9.00). There are no shipping or handling charges. There is no minimum number of books that I have to purchase. In fact, I may cancel this arrangement at any time. *Twice in a Lifetime* is mine to keep as a FREE gift, even if I do not buy any additional books.

Name _____ (please print)

Address _____ Apt. no.

City _____ State/Prov. _____ Zip/Postal Code

Signature (If under 18, parent or guardian must sign.)